N.E. McM

MOOJAG

and the
AUTICODE SECRET

Illustrations Chiaki Kamikawa

SPONDYLUXPRESS

First published November 2020 in the UK by Spondylux Press.
Profits from this book will go to actually autistic initiatives
and neurodivergent publications.

ISBN: 978-1-8380978-0-6 (print)
ISBN: 978-1-8380978-1-3 (e-book)
ISBN: 978-1-8380978-2-0 (audio)

A CIP catalogue record for this title is available from the British Library.

Printed and bound by CPI Group (UK) Ltd, Croydon CR0 4YY,
using sustainably sourced, manufactured and FSC certified Enso paper.

About the author

N.E. McMorran is a British-Cypriot autistic writer, designer and teacher, living with her teen and their rescued dog, Ben. She loves fixing things and upcycling stuff. She likes helping animals and people too. Her special interests are autism, art, natural living, and finding a solution to end homelessness. And she's a foodie, with quite a sweet tooth…

MOOJAG was inspired by her parents' bedtime stories about giant, rock candy (dad's *Gajoomstiks*) and a greedy fairy who magics-up sweet treats (mum's *Poof Poof*). The book is a reflection of her experiences growing up and the journey to her late autism diagnosis.

www.nemcmorran.co.uk
@nemcmorran

For **JAKE, CATTI, ERATO, ALEXANDER**

and all the late, self, and misdiagnosed autistics

Special thanks to my friend Trine, who read *every* draft, also editors Tango Batelli and Sonnet Fitzgerald, artist Chiaki Kamikawa, and all who offered their feedback and support, particularly the ND community on *whatsnapchatvibeinstatwitface*.

LONDON TOPS
N
W
E
S
SURREY ISLES
JUNIPER TOP
LIGHTHOUSE
BOX HILL
VIEW POINT
BOX HILL PIER
PHIL'S PHISH BAR
LEITH HILL

1

ARE YOU A REAL WORLDER TOO?

Sixteen nautical miles north lies London Tops, home before we lost Mum and Monzi.

It's ten years since the 2044 tidal surge, when Dad brought me to Box Hill Island with Gran and the others. They created the perfect Real World, so we'd be free to be different, to be *us*.

We were all gathered right here at the viewpoint when I first met Izzy and Adam. I was only three. Adam and I were the same height, but he was talking already. Izzy was barely even walking.

I stretch out in the grass, as the sun soaks the grey cells of my e-skin-covered body, and hold up my silvery hand. It glistens in the warm light. Behind it, in the distant water, fragments of a sunken skyscraper glimmer like tiny sails on the horizon; adrift in the sky, a wispy octopus-shaped cloud.

Gran says the smart skin we wear instead of clothes is 'all thanks to those colour-changing, shape-shifting cephalopods of the sea'. She never told us why she called it PIE, only that she designed it to 'free the people'. She does like to eat pies, though. How did pre-Surgers live without it? And all those homeless, how could they have kept safe and dry?

My neck tingles from my hood vibrating.

Someone's coming.

I tilt my head and glimpse a small, sparkling turquoise figure.

It's Izzy darting back from the woods, but she's headed straight for the curved stone wall beside me. I look round to scan for Adam's tall body and rainbow-coloured skin. He's still stood at the forest edge beneath the Autumnalis tree. I watch him plant his feet thoughtfully astride the snowdrops and reach up into its knobbly branches. I turn back.

"Did you see him, Nem?" Izzy calls to me. She's bent over the wall and waving her sea-blue arms in Adam's direction.

I shut my eyes, letting a cool breeze sweep my bare face. "Picking blossoms again?" I picture Izzy's scrunched-up beady eyes staring at Adam. "You *know* it's—"

"I *know*," she says, catching her breath, "—'One of the few trees that flower in hölchoko'…"

Weird to think pre-Surgers had more than two seasons.

Hölchoko sounds a lot cooler than *autumn* and *winter*.

I open my eyes to find Izzy gawking at our friend.

He's not alone.

A boy, out of nowhere, is lurking in Adam's shadow. The boy's face is pale and he looks much older than us, but his body's a *lot* smaller than ours. He's wearing clothes and, stranger still, he's floating.

Out the corner of my eye, I catch Izzy teetering to squat behind the wall. She grabs her shell-shaped Spondylux brooch from her chest and bolts back up to point the device straight at the boy. Her metallic skin sparkles as Spondylux scans the boy's short slender body.

It begins projecting a life-sized hologram of him, starting with his feet riding in black sneakers. It skims his dark-green velvet trousers, matching unbuttoned tailcoat jacket, two slight humps protruding around his shoulder blades. It detects a round smartwatch, too, dangling on a gold chain from his waistcoat pocket. And finally, a quirky black top hat with six swaying, gold letters sprung from its brim.

Izzy pulls back her hood and combs her sea-blue fingers through her scruffy peach hair while Spondylux defines the young man's features: **MILKY SKIN. SLIGHTLY UPTURNED NOSE. WIDE SET BLUE-GREEN EYES. MATTE BLACK HAIR. EXCEPTIONAL LASHES**.

Izzy crawls up to me at speed. I inch back as she inspects my face with hers. "Your eyes," she says, biting into an apple-pear. "He's got your eyes, hair too."

I glance away from her arctic crunching to check that my eyes and hair are still *exactly* where they ought to be. Izzy frowns and spins back to view the scan results.

Mum had black hair, too. Most common human hair colour. Wish I could remember her face, though. Dad never talks about her, or ever saved any photos.

SUBJECT UNIDENTIFIABLE, declares Spondylux before projecting miniature holographic possibilities, **PRE-SURGE HUMAN. WARCRAFT CHARACTER. FESTIVAL PERFORMER.**

Izzy shouts out the letters bobbing about the character's hat, "M-O-O-J-A-G. Moo jag?" The unclassified being, now balanced on one leg in yogic tree pose, just stands there with his hands clasped over his head.

"Mooooo jag," I mutter, watching a green woodpecker glide by. The snickering bird lands on a rotten tree stump by my shining feet. It twists its head to probe its razor-sharp beak deep into a crevice. I picture the ants inside, scurrying for their lives. At least this beautiful, rare bird won't go hungry today. Its cute red moustache means he's a *he*...I'll call him 'Bill'.

"Are you two *mooing*?" Adam calls. He still hasn't seen the boy now hovering upside down behind him. A wave of Adam's brown hair flops down over his forehead as he prises a frilly flower from the tree.

"A *moo* man doing the *jag*," I call past my shoulder. I jump up to gaze over the wall. Dozens of boats with visitors to the festival are docking along the pier. It'll be funny seeing Real Worlders dressed up in those scratchy old clothes.

I turn back, so Izzy'll quit poking my middle. She shakes her head at me and waves furiously at the boy now tipping his hat to us.

"UNIDENTIFIABLE SUBJECT!" she shouts to our friend.

Adam tuts, ignoring his vibrating PIE skin, and presses his long nose into the pile of soft petals in his hand. He must just think Izzy's winding him up again. "Suppose this cow guy's wearing a funny pre-Surge hat?" he calls.

Izzy and I stare wide-eyed at the stranger. Adam, grumbling at his skin turning orange, cocks his head to spy for us as the boy's shadow sneaks over his shoulder. He jumps, startled by two eyes ogling him, and leaps back. The visitor wobbles returning to the ground and greets Adam with a tidier bow.

"*Namaskar*," he says, glancing away and popping the hat back on his head.

Adam hesitates, stumbling into us as we creep closer. "*Namaste*," I say, trying the greeting from Balancize and clasping my hands. Izzy nods, punching her right fist into the palm of her left hand in Tai Chi salute.

The boy presses his hands together, too. "*Nǐ hǎo, jambo,*

kon-nichiwa..." he calls, spouting hello in multiple pre-Surge languages, "*...privet, shalom, ciao, merhaba, salam, bonjour, hola, yiasou, moni, goddag...*" We watch, amazed, as he keeps on and on until finally cheering "*...gajoom!*"

Gajoom? Don't know that one. But there's something really familiar about it...

The boy peers through squinted eyes at our faces and studies Adam's multicoloured mosaic skin. He reaches out to touch it but snatches back his hand, as though something's tried to bite it, and rummages round his jacket's inner pockets. He huffs, flinging an arm over his shoulder to pull a sack off his misshapen back. He draws out one.. two.. three thick, pencil-length, striped sticks and dares to stroke our glistening hands as he gifts one to each of us.

I glance away. It's the sugar stick Gran talked about. Her dad would always buy her one on their trips to the seaside, before the Surge. "It's rock."

"Edible rock?" Izzy asks. She raises the stick to her pouty little mouth and licks.

"You *can* eat it, but it's hard enough to break your teeth."

"That's why it's called *rock*, then?"

I lick it with the tip of my tongue and grimace at the sickly sweet taste. Adam's brown oval eyes look as though they might pop out, as we watch each others' skins shift to yellow.

"It's pure SUGAR," he says, holding out the stick between his fingertips.

I nod. "It's candy."

Izzy's skin vibrates as she coughs up a chunk. "Look!" she shrieks, gawking at the gnawed stick in her hand and rattling it in my face. "It says 'IZZY'." Adam inspects his own name, also stamped in thick violet lettering on the end of his. Cupping it behind his long-fingers, he sneaks another lick.

Gran said that the name's 'stamped right through; as much as you eat, you can still read it'. I bite off a small chunk to reveal its fractured end. Stroking the warped letters of my name, I turn slack-jawed to the suspiciously familiar Moojag character. "How do you know who we are, sir?"

"How do *you* know who *you* are, sir?" He twitches his mouth and turns from our confused stares to rummage his sack.

"Are you a Real Worlder, too?" Izzy asks him.

He glances up at her and pulls out a dusty old scroll, which he cautiously unravels. "Are *you* a Real Worlder, too?" The unfamiliar material rustles as it unwinds and finally meets the ground. It's foolishly long. We can barely see the clumsy figure now hidden behind it. He pokes his head out to read the text:

We hereby invite you to
THE ANNUAL EXHIBITION & STICKY PARTY
23rd January 2054 @ 32 o'clock
Stikleby Hall, Gajoomdom

Letting it snap up into a neat roll, he crams the paper back in his bag and hands Adam a flat, off-white, rectangular thing.

"Gajoomdom," says Adam with his questioning stare. "Is that where you're from?" Moojag grins, peering eagerly at us inspecting the familiar object. Adam holds it out on the palm of his hand. "It's the old email symbol," he says, turning to me and gently lifting the triangular flap.

"It's an envelope," I say, gazing round at the stranger.

Where *is* he from? An island we don't know? Maybe sailed over for the festival? Which would explain the clothes...but how does he have *candy*, and *paper*—when they stopped cutting trees decades ago? He *hovers* too. Even *we* can't do that. Maybe it's some future tech...or from another planet!

I look back to find Moojag spinning on his heels, muttering senseless verse, "Round or square, sour or sweet, yum yum yum, eat eat eat…" He tips his hat to us and drifts off through the evergreen shrubs, releasing the sherbet scent of their yellow flowers as he vanishes into the woods.

2

STICKY CLUES

Adam stands gawking at the forest. "What was he wearing?"

"How was he *hovering*, you mean," says Izzy, eyeing the envelope in his hand. "If he can do *that*, how come he's wearing clothes and has paper and candy?"

I shake my head. "I know, right? He didn't even have PIE. Maybe it's a letter."

Adam slips his fingers inside the envelope as Izzy shouts "LETTER" into her Spondylux.

"You *know*," I say, "those long messages pre-Surgers wrote each other on paper."

Izzy pouts at all the images beaming from her shell. "Oh yeah, 'post'. They had a lot to say, didn't they? Look— they travelled miles in cars, delivering all their words. Hmmm, what a waste of time *and* resources. What? NO— they printed their e-mails, too!"

I sigh, still thinking about Moojag. "He seemed pretty harmless." I dream a lot when problems need solving; best use of time. I picture the people writing their letters and having to wait days, sometimes weeks, for a reply. What if they didn't get one? Dad says pre-Surgers often didn't Hola back. Sometimes never! He says they were 'hypocrites for calling us rude just because we didn't speak'.

Adam pulls a little card from the envelope and reads out the text:

USE THE STICKY CLUES TO GUIDE YOU
BE THERE OR BE SQUARE!

I screw up my face and yawn. "Let's see," says Izzy, blurting "STICKY" and "SQUARE" into her shell. "Is it a 'stamp'? Is it?…Well, *is* it?"

I grab the girl by her luminous-blue, scaly shoulders. "I am trying to work, here!"

I love working. Thinking, daydreaming, planning my next move: it's all called 'work' now. Pre-surgers thought dreamers 'lazy' or 'dumb'. Real Worlders never use words like that, because we know every moment has a purpose. Even if you miss stuff, it's impossible to waste time. I might be silent or look like I'm doing nothing at all, but I'm actually very busy. We are all busy every moment of our life.

I turn to Adam, purse-lipped. "Maybe the clues will lead us to Gajoomdom."

"Sticky clues," Izzy giggles, "from *Stick*-leby?"

Adam rolls his eyes. "Can we please just work this thing out?"

"Well," I say, "since when are there thirty-two hours in a day?" At least *I'm* paying attention to the really weird stuff; someone has to.

Adam looks back at the card.

"It only says they're sticky," Izzy mumbles, trying not to laugh.

I fiddle with the stick, picturing the candy stalls on Brighton Pier that Gran talked about.

"The rock's sticky," blurts Izzy, perching on the wall. Adam smirks at her licking her finger. "Why don't *we* have candy?" she asks. He sits down beside her.

"Because," I say, nudging myself in between them, "it causes inflammation and increases disease."

Adam stands back up to look across the water. "Pre-Surgers couldn't grow enough food," he says, leaning over the wall to watch the crowd on the pier. "They had to eat more and more artificial stuff, and sweeteners were added to make it taste good. But real sugar got too expensive for most, and it made the rich sick as a dodo."

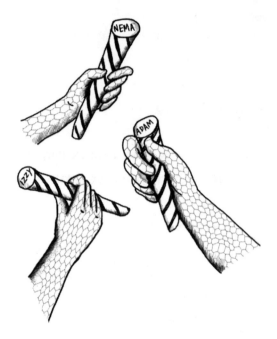

We look down at our sticks and peer round at each other. "Small dodos," I say, scanning for other Real Worlders. *Oh,* did I say dodos? "Doses! Small doses—"

Izzy sneaks me a little grin, "Can't hurt to try a bit more before they get too sticky?"

"Sure."

We start eating the candy and I notice a murky white thing poking out of Izzy's stick. She grimaces, pulling it out with pursed lips and spitting out a teeny scroll into her hand. I suck my teeth and screw up my nose at the musty bit that's jutted from mine, now Adam's too. I twist out the aged paper that's set my teeth on edge and prise it open. "It says something:

I SEE YOUR FUTURE
I SEE YOUR PAST
WHEN THE FULL MOON SHINES
YOUR HEART YOU MUST FOLLOW
FOR ONLY YOU HAVE THE POWER
TO CHALLENGE TOMORROW

"Hmm?"

Izzy waves hers in front of me. "Mine's different!" She props it up to read:

DOUBLE YOU SEE
AND YOU SHALL FIND
ME...ME!

Rubbing her forehead she leans over Adam while he reads out his:

I THRIVE IN SUN
NEAR VALLEYS AND SEA
MY STEM FUZZY
MY FLOWERS BLUE

MY ROOTS SO SWEET
THEY'RE GOOD ENOUGH TO EAT

We sit silently muddling over the funny riddles. "Wouldn't *one* clue have been enough?" Izzy groans.

"Right? What's the big secret anyway."

Adam's face strains the way it does whenever he's remembering his favourite facts. I bet he's thinking of all the plants he knows with blue flowers. "If the guy'd meant for it to be easy," he says, "he'd have just told us in the first place, wouldn't he?"

"Maybe," says Izzy, "there's more of this sweet stuff where Moojag came from." She leans into Adam wearily and peeks round at me. Her PIE's vibrating low protein and, as usual, she probably can't get food out of her head. "Should we get a little snack in, before the festival?"

I nod. My PIE's rumbling along with my stomach, and my e-skin's starting to turn. "We could do with some protein. I can barely think when I'm peachy-orange."

"Phil's?" suggests Adam. Izzy smiles, clasping her hands and checking my reaction. "I'm low on avocados, though," he says, eyeing his Spondylux.

I clock my shell and Izzy's too. "It's fine; we still have lots."

What would we do without Spondylux keeping track of what we have and what we've swapped? How did people live with money before the Real World? Dad says that hundreds of years ago our ancestors used the coral-pink Spondylus shells for coins and jewellery, and people still called money 'Spondulix' right up to the Surge. Now we have Spondylux, our personal accountant, to record what we've paid each other with what we grow or stuff we've up-cycled from junk in the sea. Who needs money anyway, when you can up-cycle almost anything into something new with your 3D printer?

I leap off the wall with Izzy as Adam sends out a Hola (that's a holographic *whatsnapchatvibeinstatwitface* to you), letting the others know we're okay. We stuff the clues in our pouches, like kangaroos, and pull up our hoods.

Breathing in the brisk sea air, we traipse off down the zig-zag path to the famous floater on the pier.

3

PHIL'S PHISH BAR

Myrta, a pre-Surge floating building strong enough to survive the fiercest storms, is now docked at Box Hill pier. It's home to Phil's Phish Bar. But she doesn't belong to Phil. Phil always says *he* belongs to *her*, because she saved him from the Surge. She has water turbines for power and an inverted solar roof to collect rainwater. Phil opens her up to shelter Real Worlders when skins need recycling and brightens chilly hölchoko days with his favourite old-Surge tunes and tasty Frank and Chips.

Bracing ourselves against the wind whistling through the cotton-ball clouds, we stride onto the pier and up to the entrance of Myrta. Above her great glass door, a string of twinkling solar lights and the glowing holographic sign 'Phil's Phish Bar'. I grab the door's chunky wood lever to tug it open, usher in my friends, and pull it closed behind me.

Waiting for the tiny water droplets to bounce off my body, I catch the sweet aroma of fried batter and steamed peas wafting past my nostrils. I pull back my hood and cross the teak wood floor to the long S-shaped bar, perching on the speckled plastic stool between Adam and Izzy. Phil stands tall behind it, his rugged body filling out his favourite metallic-purple skin. I watch his cheeks rise up to the whiskering creases of his eyes as he greets me with outstretched arms.

"Well, will ya look at that," he says in his Irish accent, "Long time, girl."

I lean in for one of his surprisingly light hugs. "How's things?"

"Everything is everything. You three?" Adam smiles and nods back as our keen DJ chef, with his twinkling glitter-beard and short bushy brows, winks at Izzy still munching on rock. "Dropped in for a Frankie, me friends?"

Izzy croaks, arching forward. "We're on a mission." Adam and I nod. "We met a little guy wearing clothes."

"Green suit," adds Adam, "and a black top hat with gold letters."

"Festival act, then?"

"He was *hovering,* though," adds Izzy. "He had *candy* too, with our names on and riddles hidden inside them!"

Phil strokes his lit, furry chin. I can't tell if he's just thinking extra hard or straining to keep a straight face. "Sounds like a wee leprechaun. What was the sprite wanting?"

Adam glances up at him, frowning. "Leprechauns hover?"

"Sure, boy—them appear and disappear at will."

Why are they talking about leprechauns? "He gave us an invitation," I say, handing it over.

Phil winks at his regulars dotted along the bar. "You're sure he had candy? The little fella sound mad as a box of frogs—" Adam presents his half-eaten rock.

Phil takes the stick and swivels it between his broad fingers. "Extraordinary," he says, shaking his head. "The boy still sound locked out of his tree," he adds, waving his fist, "like a monkey who forgot his keys."

"Definitely wasn't drunk," says Adam, finally getting the Irish slang.

"I liked him," says Izzy. I smile. Me too; pretty perfect I reckon.

"What of these riddles, then?"

Adam checks our jittery little Iz, and looks back at Phil. "We'd better get some brain food in first."

"You know yourselves. Frank and Chips for three comin' up in two shakes of the lamb's tail." He turns, grinning, to serve the young couple next to us. "Yes, me lovelies? No leprechauns tonight me 'fraid…"

Izzy giggles, swivelling round with us to gaze out the window. Soft reggae streams through our hoods, as we watch the moonlit waves lap at the boats along the pier.

"Was it only England that didn't have real fish?" I ask.

Dad says most pre-Surgers ate fake food. How could they *not* have known what they were eating?

"You mean in the '20s?" asks Adam. "They had real fish, Nem; they just weren't allowed to eat it. Made 'em eat the genetically modified stuff."

"But when the Surge swallowed up the lowlands, didn't the fake fish mutate with the wild ones?" I jump, startled by Izzy rubbing her hands and spinning back round. Three plate-sized discs cut into the bar in front of us sink down. Phil sways over, humming to the music, as the discs rise back up carrying perfectly plated pyramids of battered fish with a zesty Avocado-Pea-Lime mush and skirting of hand-cut fries.

Izzy pulls up her hood and jiggles as she tucks in. "It's not actually frankenfish, though, *is* it?" she calls out, almost yelling.

Phil shakes his head. "Come, the wee fishies mean no harm."

"But the *eyes*..." mutters Izzy, glaring back at him.

"She's not a fan of eyes," I explain.

Izzy squints back at me. "I *love* eyes...just not big, bulgy, starey ones."

"What of them riddles, now?" asks Phil.

I dig the note from my pouch, holding it up to read the text. "'I see your future, I see your past—'"

"Fortune teller—"

"There's more: 'When the full moon shines, your heart you must follow, for only you have the power, to challenge tomorrow.'"

"When is the full moon?" Izzy asks Spondylux. She swipes her finger over the hovering results: **THE FULL MOON IS ON THE 23RD OF JANUARY 2054 AT 20:08**

"That's today." Why does that date feel so important?

Phil points to a framed holographic poster at the end of the bar.

LATE ADDITION!
DON'T MISS the AMAZING MYSTIC MORAG
23rd January 7pm
Come along young and old…
HAVE YOUR FORTUNE TOLD!

"Marvellous Morag from Alba, down at last," says Phil. "She'll surely help you." He clocks the time on his Spondylux and gestures for the door. "It's seven already; don't be missin' your chance now."

I gulp my last fork of fish as I work out a fair swap for our meal. Five avocados each should cover it. "Fifteen avocados, Phil?" I ask, waving Spondylux over the bar scanner.

"Thanks a million. Let us know how you get on now, won't you?" I nod, wiping my arm across my mouth and jumping down with Adam.

"Hold on," croaks Izzy, grabbing an edible Quik-wrap. She scatters her last chips onto its smart membrane and twiddles her fingers as it vacuums into a neat package.

"Mind," says Phil, "it's fierce windy tonight." Izzy returns his nod, grabbing her little parcel and charging out as Adam drags the door closed behind us. She pouts at me and pops the parcel in her pouch.

"There'll be queues," I say, pulling up her hood. "We can't miss Morag, or we'll never figure out the clues."

"Moojag, Morag..."

"Quite like being in a rush though." I watch my arm gloss over as it self-cleans. Izzy raises her brow at me. "I mean, it feels exciting. It's exciting, right?"

"My stomach isn't excited," she mumbles back, her middle flashing yellow.

I smirk, stroking my belly and copying her permanent pout. "Indigestion, Iz?"

"She's fine," says Adam. He pauses to find his bearings as Izzy's PIE skin shifts back to its usual blue-green.

We hook arms and march down the pier. We've never met anyone from the northern peaks before. Maybe she's the only one up there, alone with her thoughts and visions. I wonder if she really can tell the future. And why have *I* ended up with this riddle, not Izzy or Adam?

4

MYSTIC MORAG

Visitors from all around Surrey Isles have flocked to Box Hill for the festival, a chance to share pre-Surge skills and trade creations.

Izzy and I gawk at the crowds: a sea of people, some animals too, in a field of lotus-shaped tents; Real Worlders in up-cycled clothes, pretending to be people they're not.

Children bounce around in reclaimed trainers with new soles made from old car tyres. Their faces hidden behind 3D-printed masks, hair woven with blossoms, dresses refashioned from oversized wool jumpers tied at the waist. A bunch of teens wearing plastic-bottle-suits swap bags with old seat belts for straps. Around camp fires, people in pre-Surge uniform: firemen, office workers, a police man, a doctor, school kids…

Adam and I peek into one of the tents as Izzy stops to catch the lingering scent of roasted pineapples. Inside, an old man in patchwork dress is teaching a family how to stitch, while a boy threads the silicone leaves from his printer tray onto a necklace cord. As I turn back, two little kids in turquoise skins chase past. They sneak up on an elderly couple to poke their bubble-wrap jackets. One of the men kneels down to let the children pop some more.

I wave Adam and Izzy on to the next tent and point up. Past the zig-zagging fabric stripes that meet at its tip is an enormous floating holographic head, a woman with dark eyes and frizzy hair poking out the sides of her black hood. The text *Welcome to Mystic Morag's Psychic Tent!* circles around it.

My heart races at the long queue. I'm not used to so many people in one place or music played outside of my hood. What'll happen in that tent? This must be how pre-Surge kids felt going to school or before they took one of those silly tests.

I press my arm, to lower my temperature a few degrees, and poke Izzy's shoulder. She mumbles something back as we shuffle into the line of chattering festival-goers. To our left, two women are crashed over a car-seat couch. One lies curled in the other's arms, eyes flickering as she dreams, while a kid gripping a car steering wheel races circles around them.

"I'll be back," Adam calls. He's spotted some kids playing Gran Turismo, their silver skins flashing yellow from overplay.

They love that game, 'cause it's the closest we'll ever get to driving a real car. Sometimes I imagine pre-Surgers whizzing round London Tops, till they've nowhere left to go. Dad says they were 'going nowhere fast'. But they must've been going *somewhere*, Dad.

I watch Adam point his Spondylux up at the hover screen, triggering the welcome message. It doesn't sound like a woman or a man's voice; I wonder if Adam's ever noticed. He taps the famous yellow wedge-mouthed circle, glowing among a string of other characters. Gripping the floating holographic stick, he launches his Pac Man through the Pac dots and munches his first ghost.

"I'll be back," Izzy hisses in my ear before skipping off to join him. I shake my head and huff, almost front of the line. Alone. Sure, I want to figure out the riddle, but what if Morag has bad news?

I look back to the tent, as a trimly dressed man with shoulder-length golden hair slips out. He flings a silk, tasseled scarf over the shoulders of his crisp white suit jacket and drapes the ends loosely around his neck.

"Hello or *no*?" the man calls. He leaps forward and peers at my face. I try dodging his piercing blue eyes, but he tilts his head with a pre-Surge royal wave and gestures for my hand. "Hello or *no*?"

I hunch my shoulders and glance away, squinting for Izzy, but he grabs my hands and swings me round. Spinning makes me so queasy; everything always ends up a blur. I feel the blood drain from my tingling face. My skin is turning yellow. I'll pass out if he doesn't stop this right now!

"Not a second time?…The end!" chants the man, pulling me back in and shoving me through the tent opening. "Step inside, love. Hello! Goodbye!"

I grab onto the pole in front of me. It's dark and musty, but something sparkles in the corner. It glows brighter and brighter, to light up a cluster of crystals on a round table and the cloaked woman sitting behind it.

"Come," beckons her gruff but kind voice, "we're expecting you."

I spot a glimmering gold-painted chair at the table and stagger over. The mystic leans forward, as I perch on its cushioned seat, and brings her rosy face up to mine to… *sniffle* me. *Ugggh*, ticklish. It's sort of nice, though.

"Is that fear I smell, dear? I shan't bite." She smirks down at the squishy-faced pug dog by her feet. It peers up at her, then round at me with it's almost-innocent, protruding eyes. "And neither does Willy, here."

I reach out to stroke the little one, but he just grunts and shuffles back between the folds of Morag's cloak. She grins, rubbing the fidgety pet with her bare foot. "So, shall we take a look at this riddle?"

She knows about the riddle. I nod. She ought to, I guess. *Knowing* is her thing. I pull the crumpled note from my pouch and flatten it out on the table. Morag whisks it up, barely scanning the words, and looks deep into my eyes.

"Well, dear, it seems only *you* can decode this delightful riddle." I drop my head with a sigh. "Shall I help you?" the woman asks, reaching across to link our hands. Why is she asking? I nod. "First, let's completely clear that little head of yours."

I frown. First, I don't know about 'little'. Second, my mind's always so busy working, plugged full of thoughts that are super hard letting go. After all, how do you tell the important ones? And when I'm not thinking, I'm usually worrying why I'm not.

See, now I'm even thinking about thinking too much! And what was I worrying about this morning? Oh, right, not giving that kid from Leith Hill enough avocados. Why can't I let go of these ugly thoughts? How did I even end up here? Right, that Moojag and his silly riddles.

FOCUS!

But how did he vanish like that? He's probably lost in the Bermuda triangle by now, like the pre-Surge planes before 3D printing that mysteriously went missing. PIE says they grew lots of Loquat fruit in Bermuda; kept the birds off the citrus. We'll have so many blackberries come kalokairi season. Oh! Now I remember—twenty-third of January was Monzi's birthday. Gran warned me never to forget my brother's birthday. I *did*.

"...must focus, girl," calls Morag, squinting at me like I'm invisible. Wouldn't surprise me. "No Moojags," she says, gripping my hand tight, "or missing planes or fruit or birthdays. Not one single thing."

What? She must have followed my entire train of thought, as though I spoke every word out loud. Did she just say *Moojag?*

"My dear," she whispers, pointing to the glimmering rocks between us, "let us empty that noggin. Focus on the crystals and count down from ten with me." I take a deep breath, filling my belly, and slowly breathe out again to count with Morag...*seven, six, five, four, three, two, one...*

I feel something I haven't felt before. Different. My head, light as a dandelion's turned to seed, could sprinkle away with the slightest puff. I feel NOTHING, but EVERYTHING. At last: no worries, no ideas, no plans. It's not a good feeling, really, it's not bad, either. It just IS.

"Good," the woman whispers, a little too close to my ear. Careful, Morag, not to disturb whatever this is. She gives my hand a feather light squeeze. "Now dear, keeping your eyes closed, tell me what you see."

5

THE VISION

Spots of colour pop up around dashes of light, as three figures appear on a boat.

"*Well*, my dear?" whispers Morag.

"Three children, a boy and two girls..."

"*Yes*?"

"They're on a long boat. There's a tower and a bright light shining all around them."

I hear Morag snort and her furry friend whimpering at her feet. "Lighthouse, perhaps?"

"Maybe. They're jumping out now…"

"Where are they, dear? What do you *see*?"

"I don't *see* anything else."

"Are you sure, girl?" Tempted to open my eyes, I squeeze them tighter. "Come on, dear, let go."

Uggghh. I take a deep breath…and I see pools of water.

"Waves, my dear. An island, perhaps?"

I huff, rattled by the constant tapping of Morag's finger nails drumming the table. "It *is* an island," I tell her, as the figures fade away.

"It's all right, dear—"

But there's another taller figure now, a woman, looking right at me. She's young with long, dark hair. I can't quite make out her face. She seems so real, but I know she's not. A ghost. But who? Morag squeezes my hand; the ghost holds out her arms as though she wants to hug me. She drifts closer. I feel my PIE's cells rise up like a gentle wave, massaging the goose pimples prickling my real skin underneath. I picture its silvery sparkle. It's never done *this* before.

"Find our boy," whispers the ghost. Her muffled words whistle through my ears. "Bring him home."

I snap open my eyes and glare at Morag, who's tapping at hers. At least she's stopped tapping the table. I shut my eyes again.

"Forgive me. I was weak, my love," continue the ghost's quavering words, "but you are strong —"

"Hello or *no*?" The over-excitable man pokes his head through the tent opening.

My heart sinks as the vision of the woman vanishes, and the hum of a dwindling crowd creeps in with the seesawing man.

Morag checks on Willy, who's busy licking his paw, and glances back at me. "It's time, my dear."

"Sorry?"

"Your time's up, dear," she says, waving her hand for me to leave.

My skin turns a melancholy-blue, as I lug my body from the chair. I want to talk about the woman, but my words don't make it out. Morag just rocks her head, muttering to herself.

Who was she? Her voice was so familiar. Am I 'strong'?

"Wats will show you the way," calls Morag, shooing me out like a pre-Surge doctor with no time. "Just follow your intuition, my dear. And regards to master Moojag…"

I stumble into an almost empty field and into the over-excitable man darting about to a band playing. "You've got a ticket to ride," he says, pointing at a black gondola bobbing on the water. "Time for your magical mystery tour…"

I turn to scan the pier and the last of the visitors returning home. Two figures astride a narrow boat are waving to me. It's Adam and Izzy. I nod to the man, avoiding his glaring eyes, and dash over to my friends. Holding out my arms to hug Izzy, I realise that's exactly how the ghost had held hers out to *me*. Just like Mum used to. Sometimes I still catch a sense of her: the sweet smell of her skin, the warm cuddles, tight but freeing at the same time. Safe. No other hug like it, not even Dad's.

I lower my arms and step up to the boat. "Missed you."

Izzy's grin must mean she's missed me too. She lends me her hand, now wearing a colourful knitted glove. "You were only in there *two hours*, Nem."

I want to laugh, smile back even, but my face is, as usual,

refusing to listen to my brain. I hold her psychedelic hand in mine and turn it round. "Why didn't you make a bag...or something more useful?"

Izzy's nose wrinkles up. I guess I shouldn't have said that.

"Well, what happened in there?" asks Adam, grabbing my other hand to pull me onto the boat.

What *did* just happen? "Well, I think I know what we're doing on *this*."

"Like?"

"The island with the lighthouse; we need to go there. But how did you two end up here?"

"Wats stuck us on it," says Adam.

"That's what I'm asking *you,*" I huff. I can't get the ghost's words out of my head.

"What?" asks Adam, scrunching up his forehead. "No, that's his name—Wats."

"One minute, I'm knitting this funky glove," explains Izzy, "the next, that guy with sparkly eyes is hurling me into a rickety old boat." Wats, the man at the tent. Morag said he would show me the way. She must have known all along.

"Morag helped me look into the future. I saw us three on the boat by a lighthouse. Then I saw this woman, a ghost, talking about a lost boy. Morag knew about Moojag, too."

We smile. There was definitely something special about

him.

"The island you saw must be Juniper Top," says Adam. "There's nothing there but the lighthouse and I doubt you'd fit a 'hall' inside it."

"She said I should follow my intuition. And right now it's saying we should go."

"Okay, then we have to."

"Er, no," croaks Izzy. "It's getting dark."

"We always trust our feelings, don't we?" Adam says, frowning down at her. "I feel like an adventure, anyway. And if it doesn't check out, we can just come straight back."

Izzy peers at me and gives Adam a nod.

"But how do we—"

"Sail this thing?" says Izzy, spying me. "No problemo. I'll be your gondolier." She twirls an arm in the air. "It's all about *thrust*."

Adam grabs a straw hat propped on the bow and sticks it on her head. She frowns, crossing her arms as I tie the hat's purple ribbon under her chin. "Right," says Adam, "Juniper Top, here we come."

Izzy leaps to the stern of the boat. "THRUST," she calls, taking charge of the oar as Adam and I squat on the narrow bench. And with a gutsy forward-and-back stroke, Izzy propels us away from the pier and Box Hill.

6

THE LIGHTHOUSE

With the moon full in the sky and solar lanterns lighting up the pier, we pass the floater and the last of the boats drifting out.

Izzy calls to a fisher trailed by a flock of squawking gulls, "Is this the way to Juniper?"

The woman, in her fluorescent-yellow skin, nods and signals to a small blinking light in the distance. "You won't find much out there, kids."

We peer out across the water to the tiny outline of an island, glimmering waves lapping softly at its shore and the beam of light projecting from a little tower. Izzy tugs the oar and steers us toward it.

"I'll take over," I say, noticing her arms shift to yellow-green. The boat sways from side to side, as I reach for the paddle and we scramble over Adam to switch places.

I feel something drag beneath the boat. "Hold on!" A massive wave rolls up and crashes down, slamming into the boat and soaking us all. Izzy drops onto the bench with a thump, sending Adam up into the air and back down with a whack, like a seesaw, as a gigantic fish leaps from the water.

"Frankie!" Izzy calls, ducking out of the mutant's way as it arches over the boat. The giant fish skims Adam's head, baring its enormous shining fangs and checking him with its bulging milky eyes. It plunges back into the sea, conjuring another wave and splashing us all over again.

Izzy peeks out from behind Adam, flicking the droplets off of his shimmering, kaleidoscopic skin. She points to a mooring post in the bay, "Dock over there!"

With the woman's words whirling in my head, I hug the oar tight and haul my orange-self back up. I steer us in and grab onto the striped wooden pole sticking out the water. Izzy seizes the rope attached to the deck, leaps out to wind it round the post, and throws the end back. Adam grabs and pulls it in tight, securing it to the boat before jumping out with me. We collapse on the soft grey sand beside Izzy and lay back to gaze up at the night sky.

"Snack?" Izzy asks, diving into her pouch.

"We just ate," says Adam.

"Like three *hours* ago." I hold my hand out to her.

"Don't blame *me*," warns Adam, "when your tums turn yellow." He gazes at the last chip. "I guess we ought to check out the lighthouse before it gets late."

"Sure," mumbles Izzy, waiting for her greasy turquoise fingers to self-clean before pulling her bottle from her pouch. She dips it in the sea, filling it with water, and waits for its osmosis magic to remove all the salt. Adam and I dunk ours in too, while Izzy swigs her fresh drinking water.

When we were little, Gran warned us not to swallow the sea water or we'd get dehydrated. 'The more you drink, the thirstier you'll be'. Dad says 'the richest one percent bought stuff as though they were drinking sea water'. The more they had, the more they wanted—even when the stuff was no good for them. That's why they were 'always thirsty and never satisfied'.

Adam slips his bottle back in his pouch and leaps up. Izzy and I clamber after him along a sandy path through the grass toward the lighthouse.

"Stop it!" cries Izzy, grabbing her Spondylux to light up the ground.

I lunge for my feet. "*You* stop it!"

"My toe!" calls Adam.

"Something bit you too?" Izzy asks, shining the torch on Adam's glowing orange legs.

"What *is* it?" I ask, afraid to look.

Izzy crouches down. "It's a crab. Aw, it's doing the dab."

"Crabs don't dab, Dizzy," Adam whimpers, gripping his injured foot and hopping on the other leg. "They wave."

I seize my Spondylux too and beam it down, lighting up a whole cast of tiny blue crabs now scuttling about our feet.

"They'll be hunting for mates," says Adam. "Saw it on PIE story. Only, this type's supposed to be extinct."

"They've been waiting for your cute feet, then," Izzy giggles.

"Let's go," says Adam, curling his lip, "before we get clawed by any more of these sexy shellfish."

I smirk, shoving Adam forward and linking arms with Izzy. "Crab favourites go first." Tip-toeing round the zippy critters, we hurtle to the lighthouse entrance and climb the stone steps to the old wooden double doors. Adam and I pull on its weathered brass knobs.

"It's locked," says Izzy, pointing to a padlock and dangling chain.

I turn my back to the door and slide down onto the step. Drawing my knees up to my chest, I drop my weary head in my hands as Adam and Izzy flop down too and huddle up to me. "How come the moon's so bright," asks Izzy, "when it's so dark out there?"

Adam smiles, gazing up at the sky. "The sun lights it up, so we can all see at night."

"The sun's gone down, though, hasn't it?"

"Just 'cause we can't see it," I whisper, with the woman's echoing voice inside my head, "doesn't mean it's not there."

"Cool," says Izzy, pouting.

Adam leans against the door, locking his fingers behind his head. "You *know* the moon's actually graphite grey, right?"

Izzy looks up at the moon frowning. "Sure."

"Sure," I answer, only hearing the woman's words, 'You are strong, my love…our boy'.

Izzy yawns long-faced at Adam and rests her head on his bony shoulder as her hood gently massages her head. "Home?"

"No," I say. "We haven't solved your riddles, yet. And what about this woman and the missing boy? 'Our boy'."

"*Your* boy?"

"Well, I don't know *whose* boy, but she was very clear about finding him and bringing him home. She seemed so real. It was like she knew me. I actually thought for a minute I was looking at myself."

"Let's get some sleep," says Adam, resting his arm round me and whispering "pillow" into his Spondylux to inflate his hood. "We'll figure it out in the morning." Izzy mumbles something as her lids flicker closed.

I try forcing mine shut, but my eyeballs feel like pebbles rolled in grit. Somehow, even with their lids shut tight, the stupid things still think they're open. "Head and feet," I mutter to Spondylux as my friends drift effortlessly to sleep. If only I could just switch off, like them. Reverse counting, that usually helps. I take a deep breath in, as PIE vibrates my scalp and the soles of my feet, and start to count back: *hundred, ninety-nine, ninety-eight, ninety-seven, ninety-six, ninety-five—*

"Ninety-four, ninety-three—"

What? My lips didn't even move! I shift my eyes. The ghost…Or have I already fallen asleep?

"Trouble sleeping, my love?" whispers the woman, leaning in and holding out her hand to touch my face. I want her to but I just shrink away. "We'll count together," she says, floating back. Her face is almost translucent, and her eyes shine bright in the moonlight.

"So close, my love; so close to finding our boy."

So tired. If I shut my eyes and just keep counting, I'll sleep. Tomorrow everything will make sense again. *Ninety-two, ninety-one, ninety, eighty-nine…*

"Eighty-eight, eight-seven, eighty-six. Sweet dreams, my darling girl. Tomorrow, we'll find our boy."

7

GLYKO RIZA

Hello. It's me, Zoe, the ghost from Nema's vision. I know, you were expecting my girl. But I've been here all along, you see, ever since that dreadful day I left them in the Surge to find Monzi. I don't think she's realised who I am yet, has she? Sometimes our feelings build up like a wall, hiding what's right in front us. I can't leave until I know they're both safe. Things are about to get dangerously sticky, and someone needs to tell the story so that Nema can focus all her energy on finding our boy. Plus, I see and hear things no one else can!

Adam has woken from the sun's rays coursing through his hexagonal cells. He glances round at the girls. Thinking they're still asleep, he springs from the steps and jogs off round the tower.

Izzy's already awake though, watching Nema's eyes inch open as she tries to shake a lingering dream. "Morning."

My girl yawns, pulling her hood forward to shield her eyes from the glaring sun. "Where's Adam?"

"Jogged off round the lighthouse."

Nema rolls over and bolts up, eager to forget the nightmare of a hundred crabs crawling all over her and the image of a petrified boy trapped inside the lighthouse. She remembers her grandmother who often dreamt the future.

Gran knew all about dreams, she thinks. *Reckoned they were useful, even when they seem silly or scary. She said if I ever dreamt about a boy I didn't know—I'd 'soon learn something very special' about myself.*

Nema takes hold of her right ankle, stretches her leg out behind her, and staggers lowering it back down.

"Not too steady this morning," says Izzy.

"Weird dream."

"That can really mess up your chi."

Nema tries again with the other leg, managing to keep her balance this time. Izzy has a go and topples over. "Looks like I'm not the only one with funny chi."

"My *positive energy* is just fine, thanks. The blue bird got me. That's all."

Nema stands on tip-toe and lifts her right leg into a

V shape. She presses her foot against the inside of her left leg and clasps her hands above her head.

"Did *you* see it?" Izzy asks. Nema rolls her eyes and shakes her head. She wants to understand what Izzy's muttering on about, but that would waste far too much energy.

"You're up, then," calls Adam, head popping out from behind the tower. "It's here, I've found it," he calls, motioning for them to come.

They head over to find him stood there with one hand behind his back. "What?" Izzy huffs, crossing her arms.

Adam brings his hand round to reveal a small bird, needle-like beak and iridescent indigo feathers, perched there on his wrist. "Bionic humming bird," he whispers.

Izzy turns to Nema, cheeky faced. "*See*," she says, gesturing with her thumb and forefinger joined in a circle, "my chi is OK." The bird whistles a little tune and flutters its wings before propelling away.

"Come on," calls Adam, sprinting off. They chase after him round the tower and up to a leafy bush. One metre tall and wide, it has hairy stems and clusters of delicately scented pale-blue flowers. "I followed her here, before."

"So?" asks Nema, sniffing the strange aroma. Citrusy-sweet, like eucalyptus and honey, smoky too.

Adam recovers the little scroll from his pouch. "My

riddle? 'I thrive in sun, near valleys and sea, my stem fuzzy, my flowers blue, my roots so sweet, they're good enough to eat.'"

"Juniper bush?" asks Izzy.

"No, Glycyrrhiza glabra: a liquorice plant. The liquorice is in its roots."

"Ohhh, *gliko riza*—sweet root," Nema exclaims, showing off the Greek words she learned from PIE story last week.

"Exactly."

Izzy captures their discovery with her Spondylux and sends a Hola. "But Spondy' says this stuff died off with the floods."

"Someone must have rescued a specimen," says Adam, excited, "planted it out here, and it survived."

"People used to fight over it," Nema tells them. "Banned like sugar when it got so rare."

"Yeah," says Izzy, pointing at the holographic results, "the Glika Wars. China used it for thousands of years to cure food poisoning and infections. Pre-Surgers used it in medicine, sweets, tobacco—"

"So we found your fuzzy plant," says Nema before Izzy recounts the entire pre-Surge story. "*Now* what?"

Izzy grips her waist feebly. "I'm ravenous."

Nema sets herself down on the ground. "Eat your

Quik-wrap."

"Saving it."

"For?"

"Emergencies."

"Is there anything to print?" Adam asks, kneeling down.

"Got some seaweed sheets in my stash, but I'm low on charge," answers Nema.

Adam calls "Sushi, times three" into his Spondylux, and pulls out the palm sized 3D printer from his pouch.

Izzy clasps her hands, eagerly watching my girl pluck a capsule from her pouch and insert it into the printer's ingredient compartment. Nema lays three seaweed sheets on the output tray as it flips out. "Got any roe popping?"

Izzy grabs a second capsule from her pouch and drops it in like a shot. The printer's extruder nozzle lowers over the seaweed, almost touching it, and begins constructing layers of rice. It pops out golden pearls of fish roe, held together by a thin gel membrane, followed by another layer of rice. At last, it draws a long squirt of smooth avocado filling across each one. Nema lifts the ends of the seaweed sheets over the ingredients to fold them up into pockets, while Adam packs away the printer. She hands them out and they all tuck in, as they watch the tide ebb and flow out to sea.

Izzy winks at Nema. "Special ingredient."

"What's that, then?" Adam asks, casually leaning back. "Brine?" Izzy squints back at him.

"Sea water, Iz," Nema explains.

"Nope, GLIKA."

Adam spits his chewed up mouthful into his hand. "You didn't!"

"I did! Just a *few* petals," gulps Izzy, screwing up her nose. "You said it was liquorice—"

"The roots," Adam huffs. "Weren't you listening in forage workshop? Not *all* parts of a plant are safe to eat." Izzy gulps again. She scratches her neck as Adam leans in to spy her data. "You've got no alerts..."

"Wrong," says Nema, "look at her skin, it's turning RED."

"My throat feels weird," Izzy mutters, gripping it with both hands.

"Like?"

"Itchy…tight."

Nema glares at Adam. *Maybe this adventure wasn't such a good idea after all*. She notices Izzy's PIE start to vibrate. She's going to keel over. Nema lunges forward to grab her, but Izzy topples to the ground.

Adam crouches at her side. "Izzy?" She doesn't respond. He glimpses Nema breaking into a sweat, her skin now turning red too. He gasps as she flops to the ground.

"Is Nema okay?" she hears Izzy utter, gazing cross-eyed at Adam.

"Not exactly." He shakes Nema by the shoulders as she passes out. "You?"

"Not...so...good, I—"

Adam gasps again for breath. "My head feels strange," he says. But Izzy's eyes have glazed over, and her lids are closing just like Nema's, and now Adam's are too...

8

GAJOOOOM...STIK!

"Earthquake!" calls Izzy, revived by the ground shuddering beneath them. She glares at Adam's skin. It's covered in a strange pink substance.

He glares back, pointing at her red fingers as he rubs his eyes and smears the sticky stuff across his face. Izzy sniffs her hand. "Strawberries and cream," she says, grinning as she skims her tongue over it.

Adam shakes his head and scans the eerie cave-like space they've woken up in. Nothing but dispersed patches of tacky, pink fuzz covering the hard ground. Cold to the touch, damp like concrete; thin stale air, hard to breathe.

"Strawbs? Where?" asks Nema, half-dreaming as she bolts up in the dimly lit place. "Where's our boy! And the lighthouse! Where ARE we?"

Ga-joooom…STIK! Ga-joooom…STIK! Ga-joooom…

"Not an earthquake," says Adam along with the unnatural thudding.

STIK!

"You heard that too, right?" asks Izzy.

Nema presses her hand to the ground. "I *felt* it—"

"It's coming!" Izzy angles her Spondylux at the great thing bolting towards them.

Ga-joooom...STIK! Ga-joooom...STIK! Ga-joooom... STIK!

I'm still dreaming, thinks Nema. *Must be.* "It's just a dream."

Izzy tugs furiously on my girl's e-skin, while Adam's eyes are firmly fixed on the looming **UNIDENTIFIABLE JUMPING OBJECT**. "We definitely *aren't* dreaming," he says, checking Izzy's shell.

Nema gasps at the bizarre creature bounding through the pink-laced, grey expanse. She's not sure whether to laugh or scream. "Is that *really* an oversized stick of candy heading our way?"

"Unless we're in that dream of yours, too," says Adam.

Izzy rubs her sticky eyes vigorously, but the image refuses to budge. The ginormous, column-shaped, purple and white striped stick is just like the hard candy from Moojag, only twenty times bigger. It's a hundred times flexier, too, and is bounding straight for them.

"Scarper!" Adam cries, shuffling back. But in his panic, he can't seem to free his hands quick enough from the sticky ground, and the thing is already towering over them. It starts sprouting smaller child-sized versions of itself. Twelve shorter, not-so-lean sticks tumble out onto the ground and ping themselves into an orderly row. Surprisingly pliable, they bend from side to side, rotating to form a neat ring around Nema and Adam, till they're boxed right in.

Adam gawks at Nema. "Where's Izzy?" She shakes her head and clings to his arm as the sticks begin a curious dance around them. They lunge in and out, coming closer with each inward leap and slowly fusing together.

"Close your eyes, Nem," says Adam, reassuringly, "and just count."

My girl is not impressed. *Like that'll help us now,* she thinks, grabbing her chest and screwing up her face in fear.

"Okay," he says, gripping her hand, "let's try panic ourselves out of it." She nods, squeezing his hand tight, because as Gran always says, 'You can't scare yourself'.

Throwing back their heads, they start yelling at the top of their lungs. They're so good at *not* freaking themselves out that they haven't noticed the icky sticks adhering to their skins. The mini-giant rock sticks have whisked them off the ground.

And Izzy, well, she scurried off into the distance, conveniently diving into a cart heaped full of old-fashioned sweets. She's right over there, see? Blissfully munching on candy; not a care in the world. She doesn't even hear her friends' muffled yelps as they're swiped away.

"IZZY! Izzy!" But every cry dissolves into the stuffy air, trampled by the quaking of a dozen more animated candy sticks now bounding alongside them. Each time the sticks land down on the sticky ground, they suction their sugary self-adhesive selves free and spring off again…

Ga-joooom…STIK! Ga-joooom…STIK! Ga-joooom… STIK!

The wheels of Izzy's cart start to roll with a jerk, sending a wave of sweets flying off the back. She grabs the sides and chokes on a vanilla toffee, whipping round to find a giant candy stick wedging itself between the handle bars. She gulps, burrowing her head into the mountain of treats. Suspecting she must be ill from all the sugar and what PIE calls 'hallucinating', she slowly pulls her head back out. But the humungous candy creature *is* there, ready to propel the cart off the ground. Izzy gawks as it thrusts the vehicle forward and bolts them through the air.

She scoops her arms round the candy to shield it from falling but loses balance and clings to the cart to save herself instead. She sighs as the sweets trail from the cart and vanish into the distance. Ignoring her flashing skin, she figures it can't hurt to have one more before they *all* fall off. And without a second thought, she plunges her face into the mound to devour another fudge and another and another…

She decides she may as well keep going, that it's a good distraction till this little 'episode' passes; they always do. Right now though, she doesn't seem too bothered either way.

9

PORTO GAJOOM

Nema and Adam are finally planted back down on the ground. Trying to squirm free of the candy robots, they peer through the gaps at a familiar figure in tree pose.

"They're super stickier from all their *gajoooom*ing," Moojag calls. He smirks back at them as the oversized candies peel themselves apart. "A candy sweat, if you will."

He turns away to scan the pink wilderness, muttering to himself as Nema puffs at a sugary wisp drifting through the air. She watches the crimson floss soar and pirouette back on itself to kiss Adam's cheek. He waves it away and watches it float up to a blue painted ceiling. It looks like a paused kalokairi sky with scattered fluffy clouds frozen there in time.

Adam picks himself up and nods to Moojag. "That was some trip you sent us on. We got nipped by these frisky blue crabs—"

"*Callinectes sapidus*," says Moojag, grinning. "The Conqip do delight in a savoury swimmer."

"Okay," Adam replies, mirroring Nema's raised brow as they edge away from the jumbo candies. "We found the liquorice bush, then got abducted by these sticky robots."

Nema sniffs the thin, oxygen-starved air. It smells of liquorice. "Then Izzy disappeared."

Moojag tips his hat to the kin of sticks bounding off. They dive through a billow of pink dust, and out of the haze springs the candy-loaded cart. A trickle of sweets cascading from it to reveal someone's giddy head.

"Izzy!"

"Huh? Yeah, I, er… You gotta try these," she says, licking the sugary traces from her mouth. She crosses her arms guardedly over the dwindling pile and looks up. "Was it real, then?" she asks, spotting Moojag. "It's *not* over?"

"*What's* not over?" Adam asks.

Izzy grunts, burying her head back in the mound, as the stick humps the cart and whisks it up into the air before tipping her out like pre-Surge trash.

"*Ouch!*" she cries, rubbing her PIE inflated bottom as the candy bounds off through another pink cloud.

Adam offers her his hand, but she's too busy scooping the

strewn sweets into her PIE pouch.

"What *is* this place?" asks Nema.

"My dear *gaijins*—strangers from the Real World— welcome to Gajoomdom." Adam and Izzy scan the unnatural surroundings, while Nema wonders if Moojag is calling them gaijin because he's part Japanese, like her. You see, in pre-Surge Japan, *gaijin* was what they called outsiders.

"Gajoom-dom?" asks Izzy as Nema and Adam grab hold of her arms to haul her up.

"Our kind were displaced here before the great flood. The Gajooms were born here."

"Gajoooom…*stik,*" says Nema.

Moojag nods and winks. "*Exactement,* Gajoooom…*stik.*"

"Those sticky live rocks?" Izzy snorts.

"Yes, the ones who ferried you from the port."

"Port?" asks Adam.

"The lighthouse—the secret gate to our world below."

"We're underground?" asks Izzy.

Moojag nods. "Deep beneath RW. Built before the floods by the Pofs for the rich Conqip Group. They knew of the troubles ahead and used their money to save themselves."

"I don't remember any port," says Nema, churning over the previous day's events in her mind.

Moojag screws up his nose. "The plant—not very tasty?"

Izzy turns to him wide-eyed. "We were *supposed* to eat it?"

"Got you here, did it not?"

"But the door was locked," says Nema.

"Why," asks Izzy, "would anyone create giant, live sugar sticks?"

"Candy producing candy...was *amusant* at first. Amusing indeed."

They shrug their shoulders and stare at him pacing, hands clasped behind his back. "The Conqip are addicted to sugar, you see. They even built their own factory to keep feeding the dirty habit."

Adam jerks his head. "What? That sounds like a seriously bad plan to me."

Nema is sure she's heard of these 'Conqip' before. She can't remember what or when, but she knows it wasn't good. *Is that what people end up doing*, she wonders, *when they have more stuff than they need?*

Yes, my love, it wasn't good; and yes, that is exactly what happens.

"*Vite vite*, quick quick," calls Moojag, rubbing his hands together. "You were very slow! We must hurry. One clue remaining?"

Nema and Adam turn to their fidgety friend. "*Moi*?" asks Izzy, pointing to herself. She peevishly digs out her note. "'Double you see," she mutters with a double blink, "and you shall find me…me.'"

"She's trying to see double," Nema explains to a foggy-faced Moojag.

He whirls off in pirouettes, urging them toward a large sunken hole in the floor. "You will see. On the double— down slide, down slide." Poking them with his finger, he nudges them each forward until they're teetering over the edge of the gaping tunnel. "Bye Bye! *Yia*! *Adieu*! *Salut*! Happy slidings!"

It looks cold and dark in the hole. Nema glances up at the fake sky, and gasps for air. "You want us to go down *there*?"

Moojag spins on his heels and tips his hat to her. "You want us to go down *there*?"

Izzy squeezes Nema's hand; Nema squeezes hers back.

"Here goes nothing," says Adam. He turns to high-five Moojag who just brushes it off and jumps back. The girls peer in after their friend as he drops down the tunnel. "It's FRUITY…" Adam's voice pings back, as he whizzes round a fluorescent spiral shoot. "Fruity…"

Moojag hovers between the girls and jabs them forward.

They fall in, landing on two circular mats, and plummet down after Adam.

"MANGO…" calls Nema, passing through a chilly stream of sweet air. "Mango…"

"Ice lollies!" cries Izzy, drooling as fruity icicles start sprouting all around.

But the icicles quickly melt into spikes. "Break 'em off," warns Adam, "or we're human smoothies!"

Nema dodges the frozen daggers, punching them out left and right. Izzy rips one off and aims it straight for her puckered mouth. "Mmmm, passion fruit!"

"She's eating them, isn't she?" cries Adam, swerving round a sharp bend. But a bright light flashes and a rainbow of colour bursts through the shoot, melting the icicles as he flies out into a great, bright white, domed room. Nema whizzes round the bend and shoots out after him across the polished floor. She skids right to the middle, stopping inside a hundred-foot-tall pillar of light that punches down from the oculus in the ceiling. *Oh, no—not the VR system, dear pre-Surge gamers, just a perfect circular window in the roof.*

Adam chucks her the pair of visors he's just printed and points to the ceiling. "Check out the old quadcopter, Nem." She holds the shades in front of her eyes and looks up. The tiny pre-Surge drone circling the empty space, flies a humungous banner:

BENVENUTI A PORTO GAJOOM!—WELCOME TO
PORT GAJOOM!

"Perfect, an actual port," says Nema, lifting her bum
off the floor and peeling away the gummy mat stuck to it.
"Let's go home."

"No!" calls Izzy, tumbling out with a skinny pink icicle
strangled in her yellow grip. "Not sussed *my* riddle yet."

"Looks like we're stuck here," says Adam, eyeing the
drone loop the room.

Nema's e-skin vibrates as a rush of heat balloons in her
chest and floats up into her head; she scuttles back for the
tunnel.

"There has to be a way out," Izzy croaks, shaking her head. She and Nema both stare at the hole magically seal itself up. They crawl beside the smooth curved wall, running their trembling fingers along it. "Moojag must have sent us down here for a reason," she says, staying strong for my girl, whose brain has just switched off so that she can breathe again. "And someone will come for us, at some point."

Adam sprints to the centre of the colossal space to search for a door. Any door. "Hey, check out the wall…" he calls back. "It's not flat."

"Obvs," says Izzy, eyeballing my brave girl who's leapt back up and is racing around the room like a crazed pre-Surge pet hamster in its wheel.

"No," he answers patiently. "Look…at the shadows."

Izzy stumbles on a ridge in the wall and runs her finger along its edge. "It's just an arch," she says, turning to Adam.

But he's watching Nema. She's found another one and is leaning against it. "Twenty-one…there are twenty-one," she puffs. "But they don't go any*wheeerrr*…"

Izzy spins round. "Where'd she—"

"Come on!" calls Adam, grabbing her by the hand. They sprint to the arch where Nema was standing, because the wall has just *swallowed* her up. They throw themselves at the arch but it springs them right away. Izzy hops forward, pokes a finger into the wall, quickly pulls it back out, and sticks it in her mouth.

"Do you have to eat *everything*?" asks Adam, rolling his eyes. "Does it at least taste good?"

"Sweet," mumbles Izzy, licking the finger. "Should we…?"

Adam turns from his grinning friend and dares to shove both hands into the wall at once. Izzy copies him, letting her arms pass right through. They stick their faces in, shoulders too, and the rest of their bodies until they're completely swamped by the wall. It seals itself over and returns to its pre-squidgy solid state, leaving the great space empty once again and the quadcopter trailing a new banner:

BUON VIAGGIO!—HAVE A GREAT TRIP!

10

DOUBLE YOU SEE

"*Shhhh,*" whispers Nema as Adam and Izzy squeeze through the other side of the goo.

They're squished in a cupboard-sized galley between the wall and a door that opens onto a dimly-lit hexagonal room. *"There's no place like home. There's no place like home…"* plays the *Wizard of Oz* clip on a loop.

A petite, full-bottomed girl with long dark hair sits cross-legged on the floor of the six-sided room, a door for each of its walls. She has purple wings that protrude through a stretched pink leotard, and her chubby webbed toes peek out from fluorescent-orange leg warmers. She strains her blood-shot eyes at a computer screen, glancing every few minutes at the smartwatch on her wrist.

"Just try to stay out of my way. Just try! I'll get you, my pretty, and your little dog too! Ah-hah-hah-hah-hah…"

The girl shrieks with joy at the new scene, pausing and replaying to memorise the lines. I've watched her secretly craft witch's costumes in the dead of night as everyone sleeps, props too, and play out the villain in her favourite film. She creates a world that feels more real to her than the real one, where she can be anyone, do anything.

Pausing the video to snack on a pile of nuts, she hears a creek. Izzy has accidentally pushed the door ajar. The girl peers round but turns straight back to the movie, tutting as she carefully splits a cashew in two. She pops one half in her little mouth and wraps the other securely inside a small handkerchief.

Adam peeks through the crack. "There's something in there...with wings."

"A bird?" whispers Izzy, activating her Spondylux.

Nema sniggers, pushing Izzy's hand away from the device. "That's a *big* bird."

"A plane?" asks Izzy, letting out a measly fart as she squeezes between them.

At least it won't smell, thinks Nema. *It's the silent ones you really have to worry about.*

Some pre-Surgers thought farting wasn't polite. You should've smelled *their* silent ones.

Nema clambers over Adam to get a clearer look. The girl is reaching for a small stick now and a thick wad of something. *It's not a bird or a plane*, thinks Nema. *Just a girl with a pre-Surge LAPTOP. And she's scribbling with a PEN on PAPER! What other cool stuff we've only ever read about might we find in this strange place?*

Sensing a draught, the creature sits up and glances over her shoulder. Noticing nothing, she quickly turns back to face the screen, shuddering as her translucent wings wiggle and pop back up.

Nema gasps. "A fairy?"

"*Shhh*—she might turn you into something," smirks Adam.

Izzy squints at him. "Fairies are real?"

"It's probably just a mask," says Nema. "Fairies are *much* smaller."

Izzy sighs, prodding her skin to stop it vibrating. "Nutrients low; need topping up ASAP." Nema returns a weak nod.

"Let's pick one and make a run for it," says Adam, scanning the doors.

Izzy bites her cheek. "What if they're locked?"

Nema looks back through the gap with Adam. Each door has different black letters and numbers stencilled on it. Adam quietly reads them out:

W-C

M-T

U-R-2-U

U-R-A-Q-T

T-4-2

"What language is it?" asks Izzy.

"They must stand for something," says Adam.

Nema reads them through, "W-C, M-T, U—"

"Double you see," blurts Izzy. "WC...*you see?*"

Nema presses a finger to Izzy's lips and whispers, "Your riddle?"

"'EM-p-TY'," continues Adam, with a nod.

"'You-are-too'," whispers Nema.

"I am too *what?*" snaps Izzy.

"Not you, Dizzy, the next one. And, 'You-are-a-cu-tie'."

Izzy smirks. "Thank-you-very-much."

Nema rests a hand on Izzy's shoulder. "Whatever."

"WC it is then," says Adam. "Lucky for us, it's out of her line of sight."

Nema nods, reassuring Izzy with a little bump and sweeping a sticky hand across her clammy forehead. "We'll be home before you know it. We've come this far, so—"

"Come on," says Adam, "while she's glued to the movie."

Nema eyes the girl's wings, so delicate looking. *But then, some of the sweetest creatures have the most poisonous sting, especially when they're scared or if someone upsets them...*

"Well, I'm off," says Adam, nudging the door just enough to slip through. He darts to the other side, barely touching the floor, as though it's covered in hot coals. Izzy grips Nema's arm, and together they tiptoe over to WC. Adam is panting to the beat of his thudding heart as he scours the door.

Nema presses his skin to stop it flashing. "Less haste, more speed."

"*Shhh,*" hisses Izzy, poking my girl's shoulder. A ping sounds with Adam accidentally triggering a tab in the door panel that releases it.

"Thirty-one o'clock—dinner time," mumbles the girl, mistaking the ping for her alarm. It's not actually thirty-one hours yet, but she swipes her smartwatch anyway, as she does every day on the dot. She taps the screen to pause the clip and levers herself off the floor, carefully tidying her wings as she stands. She skips to the door opposite, marked T-4-2, and utters some muffled words as she exits.

Nema gasps a sigh of relief as the door slides shut. "Looks like she's gone for T."

"Uh-huh. How about MT, then?" asks Izzy. "Surely that's where you fill up when you're *EMpTY?*"

"She didn't look *EMpTY*." Izzy shoots Nema a stern look. "I just mean—the more you eat, the bigger your stomach gets, the hungrier you feel."

"Know *that* one," says Izzy, checking for PIE alerts.

Nema crosses her arms. "Can't be that time again *already*."

"Fast metabolism."

"You sure you're not just over-stretched?"

Adam huffs. "She could be back any minute—and go in WC."

"How come?...*Oh*."

"Come on. It's open!"

Izzy giggles. "Wonder what we'll dig up next?"

Nema sniggers. "A toilet? Just a wild guess."

They step in and gaze round the small, circular room. Izzy turns with a sigh as the door clicks shut behind them. Planted at the room's centre is an enormous toilet-shaped bowl. It *is* in fact a toilet but not the usual sort.

"Well, it *is* a 'water closet'," says Nema showing off her PIE story knowledge.

You see, WC is short for water closet. That's what people used to called the little room with a flush toilet in it. You probably use one if you still live in a concrete box or don't yet wear PIE.

Izzy walks up to the gigantic loo and stretches up on tiptoe to peer inside. "Check it out; there's no bottom!"

"There wouldn't be, silly; nobody's using it," says Nema, still thinking about dirty pre-Surge toilet habits. She edges forward, hesitantly hooking her fingers onto the rim to pull herself up, and leans over the bowl.

Adam sulks. "I miss RL."

"This is real life too, Adam," says Nema. "A slightly stranger one."

"Come look," says Izzy.

He steps up to the bowl and there, emerging from the swirling water, pops a spectacular multi-coloured iced ring doughnut! It hovers toward them, immediately followed by another, identical.

"*Not* a toilet," confirms Izzy, waving her Spondylux as a whole baked LASAGNE flies up out of the whirlpool. "I'm thinking of stuff, and it's coming out!" she cries.

"Watch out," Nema calls, "here come's another one!" Adam ducks to avoid the incoming dish as Izzy leaps out of its way. *It's like a pre-Surge vending machine*, Nema thinks, squeezing her eyes shut, *except it's shaped like a toilet and you can get anything you wish for!* She quickly posts the discovery to PIE story. "I hereby name this thing 'Vending Wish Loo'."

"Couldn't you have wished for something smaller, Iz,"

says Adam, "a snack even?"

Nema fixes her eyes back on the churning pool. "Go on Adam. *You* wish for something."

What if it's not just food? Nema wonders. *What if we could wish ourselves out of here?*

The water begins to swell. They watch it rise up out of the bowl and hurl every single treat the girls wished for with one great heaving purge. Izzy hurriedly darts about, hoarding the showered edibles as Nema and Adam take cover.

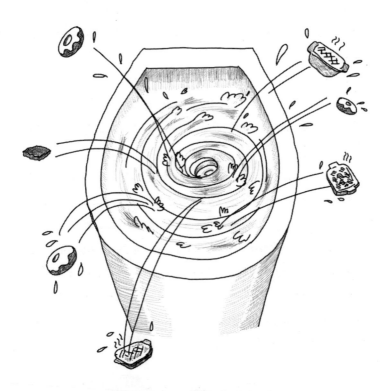

"Namaste!—*Namaste!*" hail two identical Moojags bobbing up from the bowl beneath drenched top hats.

Izzy gulps the last bite of a brownie and forces a shepherd's pie into her PIE pouch. "Moojag," she mumbles. "TWO of you?"

"NEVER," he answers. "There is only ONE Moojag." "*Never,*" confirms his other. "*There is only ONE Moojag.*"

"Which of them is the *real* one?" whispers Izzy.

Adam checks for differences. "They're exactly the same."

"Double you see, chip chop. Won't do to be late for the party!—*Double you see, chip chop. Won't do to be late for the party!*"

"Chip shop?...Party?" Izzy chirps. "*Chip shop?... Party?*" her own voice echoes back at her.

"Izzy?" says Nema, examining Izzy's double, beside herself. "*Izzy?*"

"Nema?" says Izzy, glaring at an identical Nema. "*Nema?*"

Adam turns to face his own other, as though looking in a mirror. "Hello?—*Hello?*"

"Are you me?" asks Adam. But the double turns his back on him. "*Are you me?*" Adam turns again—his other follows.

Nema scans the room and notices the mirrored walls all around them, while Izzy chuckles at the hilarious picture of their tall, confused friend scratching his head and his double continuing to copy him.

"Please, no," groans Adam, shielding his ears from the giggling girls' echoes, "not FOUR of them—*Please, no... not FOUR of them.*"

"Jump in and let's go!—*Jump in and let's go!*" exclaim Moojag and Moojag.

Izzy grimaces. "Eeew, not in there—*Eeew, not in there.*"

"Can't take any more of this repetition," says Adam. "*Can't take any more of this repetition.*"

Moojag and his double, both in tree pose above the swirling water, begin to count, "One—*one*, deux—*deux*, tria—*tria,* quattro—*quattro*…" They command the water with swooping hands. "And DOWN we go!—*And DOWN we go!*" It spins rapidly and rises up over the edge before sucking them both in.

Nema climbs over the rim of the super-sized toilet. "Come on!—*Come on!*" Adam gives Izzy a leg up, and they jump in after Nema, like human ingredients churning in a human-sized blender.

And they're gone.

The toilet has swallowed them up.

11

CAMOUFLAG-ATION

Appearing out of a giant funnel, they slide one after the other onto the ground in an altogether new place.

"Hello or *no*? 'Cause tomorrow never knows—"

"Quit talking in riddles, Wats; you'll frighten our guesties away." Moojag adjusts his sodden waistcoat and whacks his soaked top hat against his thigh. "After all," he says, startled by the hat popping into shape and the floppy letters springing back up, "they've travelled such a way."

Wats, still dressed immaculately in white, drops cross-legged onto the red-bricked path beside the dishevelled friends. He chuckles, flicking a lock of hair from his face. "Took the long and winding road, did we? Down the helter skelter, was it?" Jumping straight back up, he turns and skips along a path between the little, violet-flowered bushes.

Moojag bows apologetically. "We're not *all* goo goo, you

know."

Wats swings back and forces a wink. "Most, darling Mooj, are quite up there." He points to the new sky-painted ceiling. "You're not nearly as normal as they'd have you believe. Walrus knows best, goo goo Gajoom—"

Moojag stamps his foot, startling Wats but not the distracted Real Worlders. They're too busy checking out the prettier but still peculiar surroundings to notice the bizarre conversation. They're just grateful to have survived the toilet.

Izzy jerks the water droplets off her e-skin and eyes the two characters. "Where are we?"

"Stikleby," Moojag and Wats answer, knocking each other with a mutual bow.

Moojag adjusts his hat and wobbles over to a pile of long, thick, stripy tubes. "Hurry, Real Worlders, put on these before you drown in a puddle."

Izzy frowns. "Can you drown in a puddle?"

"Quite you *can*," declares Wats, flapping his arms and feigning to drown. "Think for yourself, dizzy miss Izzy."

Nema recalls a nursery rhyme Gran told them when they were small about a doctor who had 'stepped in a puddle, right up to his middle'. He didn't drown, obviously, but he never ever went there again. *Will WE ever come HERE again*, she wonders, *if we ever make it back home?*

Adam inspects the funny looking tubes as Moojag lines them up precisely in length order.

"Camouflagation," explains Moojag. "You will be undercovering from here on."

"If they catch you," adds Wats, "you'll wish you *had* drowned in a puddle."

"*They*?" asks Adam.

"And why *us*?" Izzy calls.

"We'll get to it, my friends," says Wats, tossing Adam the longest tube.

Nema picks up the medium sized one. "You want us to wear this? Is it like e-skin? We'll look like those funny sticks."

"Ain't she sweet?" calls Wats, nodding in sync with Moojag. They cross their arms, waiting for Izzy to collect her tube as Nema and Adam search for an opening in theirs.

"Please, allow me," says Wats, snatching Nema's tube and pulling it over his head. He lets it fall to his feet before flinging it off again and lobbing it straight back at her. "Slip it on," he says. The friends glance at each other before cautiously donning the white and indigo striped skins.

"Help!" screams Izzy. "I can't see."

Wats chuckles, peering through the invisible mesh spy

holes of her costume. "Hello or *no*? It's back to front, baby. Spin it round."

"I see now," she calls as a faint giggle escapes Nema's suit.

"That's all right," says Wats. "Glad it's all over!"

"You can see out, but no one can see in," explains Moojag. "But stay quiet, for no Gajoom in the history of Gajooms has ever had the gift of voice."

Nema squints at him through the mesh. "You mean, they can't talk?"

"No clever remarkings from you, young lady. They have not a humour in them."

"They have no sense of humour, you mean?"

Wats huffs, slumping back on the ground cross-legged. "Too much monkey business!"

Adam nudges Nema's middle through the costume with his elbow. "*Okay*—I'm sorry," she says in as loud a whisper as she can muster.

Moojag pirouettes round the friends. "If they detect difference, they'll capture you and—*POOF*—that will be that."

"Who'll capture us?" Adam mumbles, afraid of irritating Wats any more. Moojag presses his hand to Adam's chest and perks his ear up against him as though superglued.

"Why do you want us looking like those silly sticks?" asks Izzy.

"Well, this place is ruled by the Conqip Group," explains Wats, "the top one hundred richest before the surge. Then, there are the SuperAuts who created the Gajooms and keep to themselves. And, of course, there are the Pofs who keep the place running tip-top."

"Pofs?" asks Izzy.

Moojag finally releases his ear from Adam's side with a grin. "The girls brought here by the Conqip to build their empire, super strong. The poor things think they can do magic; some believe they're fairies with their wings and all. Brainwashed. Very sad."

"We saw one on the way here," says Nema. "She had these amazing purple wings. She was so busy working, she didn't even notice us."

"Kitty, in the Switching Room?" asks Wats. "The room that leads to all parts of Gajoomdom? Except MT, of course. I doubt you'll have need to go in there, though."

"She was watching a pre-Surge film," says Izzy wide-eyed, "and writing on paper."

"Sounds like Kitty, all right," says Wats. "Poor darling, fed fake food and terrible lies like all the rest. They depend on the stuff."

"If in doubt, feed 'em, feed 'em..." chants Moojag.

"*Feed* them?" asks Nema.

"A Pof will do *anything* for food, don't you know?"

"Friends, the exhibition is about to start," calls Wats. "They'll be zooming all about the place in a mo."

"And the sticky party?" whispers Izzy.

Wats jumps in front of them. "Sure, always sticky, full of cheeky Gajooms just like you!" He demonstrates a Gajoom move with a crouch down and frog-leap forward. "All together now."

Adam clings to the inside of his narrow tube and has a go at Gajooming. Moojag tips his hat to Nema and Izzy as they wriggle apart and start bouncing all around.

"Natural 'joooomers," says Wats. "Won't be long now. Courage all and good luck."

"*What's* the plan?" asks Nema, peering at him through her spy hole. "*Why* are we pretending to be candy robots?"

Wats turns back with a wink. "Charlie will deal with all the peculiars. It was she who sent us to find you. She looks after the Pofs, since the Conqip have no care for women's things. She curates the annual exhibition. Wonderful stuff. Keeps the Pofs entertained and nicely distracted."

"You have the special genes," says Moojag, hovering beside them. Izzy nudges Nema.

"Are you sure you've got the right people?" asks Adam, edging up his disguise.

"Well, if *you're* not sure, how can *we* very well be?" poses Moojag, pulling the disguise back down.

"But *you* were sent to find *us*," says Adam, irritated.

Moojag peers down at his own reflection in a pool of water. "So you *are* sure."

"He's a blast, isn't he?" says Wats, springing up to punch the air. He looks round, cocks an ear, raises both arms, and air drums to the growing sound of a triumphant orchestra. "That's our cue, goo goo Gajoom. All you need is LOVE, la la, laaa, do do, dooo…"

Moojag performs a pirouette, bows and waltzes off, coat tails flying as his frail body fades into the distance. "Has he left?" asks Adam. "He didn't say goodbye."

"Oh, darling! Never does. Never will."

"I guess," suggests Nema, "he just isn't into goodbyes. Never saw the point, myself."

Izzy nods. "People sure like 'hellos' down here, though."

Wats skips round her, grinning. "It's not the last you'll see of him." Izzy and Nema share a relieved smile. They've grown quite fond of the boy. Of course.

Wats guides them a little way along the path. "Just follow the sound of the trumpets till you reach the little golden bridge at Stikleby Hall. Charlie awaits you there. You must *stik* on the pads to enter." Adam nods under his disguise, as Nema attempts a thumbs-up under hers.

"It's been a hard day's night," says a drooping Wats. "I'll be on my way." He tosses his hair and bolts off in the opposite direction. "*Au revoir,* as Moojag would have it, or *not*!"

12

STIKLEBY HALL

Izzy shuffles up to Nema as Adam leaps with an awkward *Ga-joooom* and firm *STIK* down. "I hope this Charlie tells us why we're here," she says, "and gets us out of this sticky mess."

Adam turns back with a jiggle. "On three, just jump, okay? One...two...THREE!"

The girls leap and land two feet forward with a wobble. Nema goes for another one, leaving Izzy wriggling behind on the spot. "Unstick yourself," she calls, watching Adam pluck his feet up and peel his costume from the ground. Izzy grimaces at the layer of gooey pink gunk bonding to her feet. She lifts each foot slowly off the ground.

"I see the bridge," calls Adam, continuing down the paved path by a little stream. Nema waits for Izzy to *Ga-joooom...* *STIK* up to her, and together they bound off after him.

It's like watching a pre-Surge potato sack race. Or is it

the three-legged? I'd cheer for them, but they can't hear me.

"There'd better be food," says Izzy.

"Good luck with that, mesh mouth," answers Nema.

"Hey, there it is!" cries Izzy. "That must be Stikleby Hall."

Adam bounces back to their side and hisses through Izzy's mesh, "*Shhhh!* We don't talk, *remember*."

"*Yes*, but how'll we—"

"Right," says Adam, "we need a signal to communicate with each other."

Izzy cocks her head, gawking at Nema who's bent over sideways. Isn't my girl elastic?

"We might miss that," says Adam, "without our peripheral vision."

Izzy squints at him. "You have *animal* vision?"

Nema bumps her friend. "Not '*feral*'. He means we can only see straight ahead in these things."

"That's *it*," exclaims Adam. "We'll nudge each other. Once for 'yes', like this—" He sticks his bum out, giving Izzy a little jolt.

"Hey!"

"And twice, like this—"

"Watch it," warns Nema, flexing to avoid Adam's second blow.

"For 'NO'."

Izzy scuffles about inside her tube to cross her arms. "But what if we're nowhere near each other?"

"Gajoom on the spot?" suggests Adam.

"Okay."

"Nema?"

"Yes, all right. But let's not go *nowhere* near each other." The kids carry on up the path to the glistening bridge and pause for a moment to catch their breath.

"HELLO THERE!"

Nema peers over the bridge to locate the firm but filmy voice. A tall woman wearing a trim, gold-satin suit and grape, velvet pumps is waving excitedly at them. Behind her, a red brick building stretches all the way to the fake sky ceiling. It looks like an eighteenth century mansion with three arched, glass doors at its centre. Adam bounds over the bridge with his friends close behind.

The woman smiles through pinched lips and primps the petals of a purple rose pinned to her jacket breast. "Do you love your costumes?" she asks, gently brushing back her tousled, silver hair from her pale, round face. "I'm so excited to have you with us for this year's exhibition; it's my finest yet. I suppose you must be tired from all your Gajooming?"

Adam shuffles beside her. "It does take it out of you."

"Ah, you must be Adam?"

"Yes," he says, nudging Izzy, "and this is—"

"Hello, Izzy," she says, poking the smallest Gajoom. "Delighted to finally meet you."

"I'm Nema."

Charlie smiles. "So you are." She darts to the wall and presses her hand against the biometric reader below a plaque that says: **STIKLEBY HALL**.

Three big circular discs rise from the ground as Charlie calls the friends over. "You'll join the Gajooms and wait there till I announce the exhibition winners. Remember though: not a word."

Recalling Wats' instructions, they leap straight onto the discs. Nema giggles, reminded of Phil's Bar. She pictures them dished up like Frank and Chips, and wonders whether Charlie would get her Real World humour. She decides not to share the joke.

"You've been well informed, I see," says Charlie with the doors swinging open into the great hall. "Stay cool, be Gajooms, and remember not to talk unless it's just us in the room." She taps her ear. "Whenever I do *this*, it means it's time to go."

Izzy leans toward Nema and nudges her twice. "Go where?" asks Adam. "What's this all about? Why did you bring us here?"

"Sorry, really must go." Charlie darts into the hall, glancing back with kind but tired eyes. "I'll explain," she calls, "but the Pofs and Gajooms will be getting impatient. They're quite unpredictable when their routine is changed."

Nema and Izzy nod inside their suits, while Adam struggles to imagine what sort of feelings a stick of rock might have. Then again, giant animated candy is hardly normal, is it?

Charlie presses her hands together and tilts her head. "Just stay low, mingle in, and follow my cue."

"OK," calls Izzy, already forgetting her quiet voice.

The Gajoom-camouflaged friends bound into the hall after Charlie, stopping inside the doors to take in the dazzling room: shiny marble floor and gold-leafed walls. They gaze up at four huge glass chandeliers hanging down from a blingy, gem-studded ceiling. Izzy gawks at their crystal globes lighting up the hall like hovering phosphorescent jelly fish. Nema guesses Izzy thinks they're real pretty. She thinks she might understand, now, why Dad used to yell so much at Gran about gold cars, yachts, and babies' slippers studded with real diamonds. Izzy can't see Nema's face, but she has pictured her friend's pout and furrowed brow perfectly.

Adam leaps from side to side nudging his friends. Two very large Gajooms are headed their way.

Ga-joooom…STIK! Ga-joooom…STIK! Ga-joooom…

13

TAKING THE CREDIT

...STIK! Ga-joooom...

The friends freeze in the hall's entrance as two ten-foot-tall stripy sticks bound right up to them, then immediately veer off into a sea of Gajooms at the centre of the hall. Izzy cups her mouth at the sight of a gold-covered eagle mounted on the wall, but her friends' eyes are still stuck on the bendy Gajooms. The sticks appear to be greeting each other, twisting at their middles and locking together like giant puzzle pieces before unwinding back to their usual upright selves.

Nema and Adam twist around each other to try out a quick Gajoom hug. They wiggle up to Izzy to share one with her too, but a drum roll gives them a fright, and they jolt back upright. The anthem they heard earlier plays out again, with all the sticks making for the front of the stage. Adam nudges Nema, Nema nudges Izzy, and they slip in with a bunch of

Gajooms to the side.

"Welcome, dear Pofs and Gajooms, to our tenth annual exhibition," Charlie calls, reappearing up on stage. "Today, I have the honour of presenting the magical work of our amazing Pofs. And this year, a few Gajooms have even taken part." She directs the feverish crowd to the gold-framed pictures covering the walls all the way up to the ceiling.

The Gajooms bounce up and down, thudding the ground with excitement. They duck as a cloud of Pofs, flapping their iridescent wings in cheer, whiz into the hall and sweep over them. Nema and her friends spring up and down to blend in with the Gajooms, until the raucousness finally fizzles out with another drum roll and Charlie continues her speech.

"As ever, incredible work." Charlie pauses to scan the eager crowd. "It's a competition. Of course, not all can be winners." She turns and hands a scroll to a curvy Pof with purple-tinted wings. She's different from the other girls, Nema guesses: older. She has short, fuzzy, black pepper hair and a pair of cat-eye spectacles balanced daringly close to the tip of her nose.

"Poof Poof, will you kindly do the honours?"

"Yes, Charlie, darling." The Pof snatches the curled document and wraps her effervescent rainbow scarf even tighter round her neck. Charlie nods, gesturing for her to reveal the winners. Poof Poof turns sharply to face the crowd.

"Thank you! Thank you!" she calls, bowing and squinting as she nudges the glasses up over the bridge of her nose. "Darlings, how creative. You must have worked hard to produce such a magnificent art."

Nema, perspiring inside the disguise, fumbles to press her skin and lower her temperature while Gajooms stand motionless and Pofs swarm overhead.

"You *should* be thrilled, my darlings, the rewards are delicious!" Poof Poof pauses as the 'anthoom' they heard earlier plays out again. She peers over her spectacle rims and licks her entire upper lip. "Marshmallow banoffee waffles with lashings of maple syrup and salted-caramel popcorn trees!"

The winged girls go bananas. Gajooms wiggle on the spot, while Pofs whiz about in figures of eight. A horn blares, silencing the room. Izzy rubs her hands together, grinning; she doesn't know what any of that stuff is but guesses it tastes incredible.

"In third place," Poof Poof calls over the incessant drum roll, "G21. It's a Gajoomdom first, my darlings. We actually have a *Gajoom* finalist."

The sticks jump up and down, thudding the ground as the winning Gajoom bolts onto the stage. Two muscly Pofs, gripping the top corners of a painting, swoop in like super-charged cherubs and lean it against the podium. Charlie accepts a bronze medal from Poof Poof and gently presses it onto the Gajoom's sticky form. Nema recognises the bold picture of two white lily flowers. She's seen it on PIE story, and it was painted by an artist called Georgia O'Keeffe.

My girl's so good at remembering pictures; though she can't remember my face.

Glancing at the art across the walls, Nema realises they're *all* by famous artists; most are over a hundred years old. She zooms in on the painting. *Okay, sure, there are animals who like to paint but come on—not a stick without hands, or even feet!*

Izzy glares at the graceful flowers and gives Nema a double nudge. They often learn together because they love the same things, and she knows her artists pretty well too.

"And in second place: my Kitty Poof." The winged girl they managed to avoid in the Switching Room hovers onto the stage. Kitty adjusts the pink bum-bag that's worked its way round her middle and lands with a wobble beside the podium.

"Congratulations, pussy cat," says Poof Poof, hanging a silver medal on a pink ribbon around the girl's neck.

Charlie calls four other Pofs to the stage. They haul a

large black and white painting through the air, skimming the Gajooms as they head for the podium. Nema instantly recognises the famous squiggly pattern and squints her eyes to focus on its hypnotic curvy lines. The Pofs lean the art against the podium and teeter off, flapping their wings excitedly as the picture's long stripes start to vibrate.

Bridget Riley painted this picture in 1964, she called it 'Current', and it really does move—if you stare at it long enough. Some people can even see colours in it.

Kitty fondles her polished medal, running her finger over the name inscribed on it, and rocks her head. "Dorothy! Not Kitty."

"Dorothy! Dorothy!" cheer the four crazed Pofs, still buzzing around Kitty grinning with delight at her audience. She spins round then falters, landing with a muted thud on her well-cushioned behind.

Poof Poof swoops in to drag her off the floor. "Yes, of course, darling, 'Dorothy' it is." Glaring at the mellowed sticks in front of the stage, as Kitty flashes her medal, she orders one to fetch her sweets. It swivels round and leaps off through the dividing sea of Gajooms.

Grimacing at Kitty mumbling something about a witch, Poof Poof returns to the podium and pulls a card from the final envelope. "And in 1st place: G9-8-4. *Nine hundred and eighty-four*?" The cheering stops. She glances suspiciously at Charlie who's tapping an ear and winking at some Gajooms beside the stage.

"What is this? There is *no* such Gajoom!"

"Yes," explains Charlie softly, "that's because *they* are THREE."

Nema bumps Izzy, who nudges Adam, who almost topples over nudging them back. They wiggle between the Gajooms and hop toward the stage: Izzy shaking, Nema wondering why Charlie would take such a risk, and Adam hoping this plan actually leads them out of the batty hall and their muggy ga-jump suits.

"This year we have three joint first-place winners," Poof Poof informs the audience.

The crowd goes berserk at the extraordinary news as Charlie calls on two Pofs nattering in the corner to fetch the winning art work from the wall. The other Pofs fly haphazard, while Gajooms pound the ground disturbingly out of sync.

Charlie welcomes the three friends stalling at the platform. "That's right, *leap* on up and claim your medals—9, 8, and 4!"

Nema shuffles back, bends down low, and throws herself up onto the first step with a wobble. She goes again, making it onto the second and finally onto the stage. Adam follows, flying up like a gravity-defying slinky. Izzy just freezes on the spot. Poof Poof shoots Charlie a fierce look, while Izzy closes her eyes. I imagine she's imagining waffles. Adam and Nema cross their fingers and wince as Izzy hurtles in one giant leap like a fish out of water onto the stage. She springs upright and quickly huddles into line with her friends.

A gang of little Pofs gather round the small winning picture deposited on the stage. They frown, chattering among themselves, inspecting the colourful portrait of a woman with dark braided hair and thick brows that almost meet in the middle. She's seated in front of tropical leaves. A still hummingbird hangs from her thorny necklace, and a spider monkey and black cat crouch over her shoulders.

Poof Poof turns from the winners to eyeball Charlie. "Which of them is which?" Kitty's face lights up. She glances at Poof Poof before turning to jab Nema in the stomach. Adam leaps between them.

"Our wondrous winners," calls Charlie, skipping to Nema's side. But my sweet Real Worlder is lost in the mysterious painting.

She guesses from the way the woman looks right out of the picture, it's a self-portrait. She figures that the woman is strong and brave from the scratches left by the sharp thorns around her neck. *I bet she survived terrible things, and making art was what saved her.*

She didn't have the easiest life, my love, but she never gave up and was always true to herself. Her name was Frida Kahlo.

Charlie claps her hands in the air, firing up the rowdy Pofs into an unexpected roar and shocking Nema into a bow. Poof Poof waves to the crowd as Charlie guides our disguised Real Worlders off the stage, through an arched doorway, and out of the great fizzing hall.

"Quite unsavoury," says Poof Poof, glaring at Charlie as she hovers alongside her down the corridor.

"Sorry?"

"A recount, at once!"

"It was all fair, and Kitty was a winner, wasn't she? Really, Poof Poof, it isn't worth the bother."

"Perhaps not, but—"

"Don't you have tastier matters to attend to?" Charlie asks with a wink.

Poof Poof squints, straining to make sense of Charlie's comment. "Of course, yes! We must celebrate *tout suite*. Yummy delights for you, my darlings," she says, zooming back on herself to brief the winners, "I know exactly what you crave."

Izzy's mouth waters at the thought of waffles, whatever those are, and the most shockingly curious part—she's done nothing to *earn* them. Adam worries how long they can keep up the act. Nema can't decide whether she's excited or terrified.

Poof Poof hovers toward a large circular opening in the wall at the end of the passage. "In here, darlings." She drops inside with Kitty and waves down Charlie after them.

Nema nudges Adam twice. He nudges her back and hops through the hole, sliding down after Gajoom 21 into a ball-shaped room. Izzy and Nema slide down after them into the smooth, round space and huddle at the centre of its upward sloping floor.

Poof Poof whizzes back and forth, wagging her little wand. "I don't know how the Gajooms pulled it off, Charlie. But let's reward them anyway." She lowers the wand and squints over at Charlie stooping with her heels pressed up against the curved wall. "*Helloooooo?*...Charlie?"

"Yes, of course." she answers, directing Poof Poof's quivering wand away from her face.

Nema senses a trap. *Do Gajooms eat? And if they do, it's certainly not the way WE do it!*

Poof Poof loops her wand, "One, two, three, pif...pof... POOF..." A burst of pink smoke fills the entire room. Out of it floats a small tree of caramel popcorn. Poof Poof sneers at them all, turning to face her daughter. "Kitty is first, of course."

Kitty dives through the haze to claim her treat and flies back to the top of the room. Cradling the branchy cluster in her arm, she prises a single nugget and pops it in her mouth.

"Now, back to our unlikely winners." Poof Poof whisks her wand vigorously in the air, filling the space with yet more candy cloud. Between the foggy patches, she catches a glimpse of a sluggish Kitty, a crouching G21, and Charlie poking her ear.

Nema spots Charlie, too. *How does she expect us to escape undetected from a room with sloping walls?*

Charlie waits for the pink stuff to block Poof Poof's view, slips over to their side and signals to the floor. But as the friends bend to look down, the floor opens up and they plunge to a cushioned galley below.

Charlie doubles over as the secret opening, now above them, seals closed. "Hurry! When she sees we're gone, we won't just be *eating* floss."

Adam squeezes his eyes shut and opens them again to see better in the dark. "I like an adventure, but is this *really* necessary?" Nema glances at the Gajoom who's fallen down with them and shuffles behind Adam.

Charlie smiles, poking the rigid stick. "How rude of me; I almost forgot to introduce you. This is dear Biermont, previously known as 'Conqip IV', but he couldn't hurt a fly."

Nema shuffles back, peering at the ground. *It's pretty hard not murdering ants, there always being so many. But flies? No, it's not that easy to 'hurt a fly'; near impossible catching one.*

Izzy, still dreaming about her unclaimed prize, totally misses Charlie's introduction and the Gajoom's stripes curl up to reveal a tall, bald guy waving at them.

Nema notices he has smile wrinkles, just like Charlie's, hooking his eyes and mouth. *He certainly doesn't LOOK like he would hurt a fly, even if somehow he ever DID manage to catch one.*

Izzy groans, scouring her vibrating pouch. "Guess I had enough sweets—"

"Come along," Charlie calls back, steering into a long shallow corridor, G21 and Adam darting behind.

Izzy crouches inside the disguise to cradle her head in her hands. "Is anyone going to tell *me* what's going on?"

"Didn't you see him?" Nema clicks her tongue as she bends down to hoist up her tube, so she can move freely again.

"Huh?"

"Never mind; let's go."

14

SUPERAUTS

"Wait for us!" calls Nema, scurrying down the passage with Izzy.

The others have hit a dead end, standing by a stone stairwell that curves up and round; above them a glowing sign reads: **S.A. LAB**

Izzy grabs her Spondylux as they approach. She shakes it and sighs when it doesn't boot up. "Isn't an S-A something pre-Surgers wrote?"

"That's an *essay*, Iz," says Nema.

"That's what I said." Izzy sighs, fiddling with her inactive shell.

"It stands for SuperAut," whispers the ex-Conqip.

Izzy glares at Adam. "What happened to your voice?"

"Wasn't *me*, Iz."

Charlie turns to point at the wall and draws a wide circle in the air. A round panel pops out and rotates up to reveal a new opening, this time onto a vast brightly-lit room. "Welcome to the SuperAuts' lab," she says, briefly blocking the glare as she steps through.

The friends glance at each other and teeter by the window to stare into a big room with whitewashed walls. It looks like a pre-Surge classroom and smells a bit like those old hospital wards. The unfamiliar hissing sound of fans whirring, and fingernails tapping furiously on plastic, rings inside their Real World ears.

"You'll see," says Biermont, shifting up his disguise.

"It's okay," says Nema, nudging her puzzled friend. Izzy glances at the stranger's pin-striped trousers and down at his shiny loafers as Adam and Nema clamber past.

"I was a Conqip," he explains, offering Izzy his hand to help her through, "until I found out what the others were up to." The man peers down the corridor and hops through the hole after her as the panel morphs back into the wall.

"Working PCs," hisses Nema.

"Macs!" cries Izzy, shuffling behind her into the room full of grinding pre-Surge computers.

"*Shhhh—*"

Charlie smiles. "It's okay, you can talk in here for now."

Seated behind twenty-one perspex cube stations are twenty slight, long-haired teens. Some wear super soft, loose-fitting cashmere tracksuits; others, figure-hugging stretch-cotton leggings and tops. Like Moojag, their pale faces and focused expressions make it hard to tell their gender or age. But they're much taller than him and certainly older than Nema and her friends.

Most wear chunky headphones to drown the buzz of the computers or muffle the incessant chatter of an over-excitable neighbour. Some wear special tinted glasses to correct colour difference; some to help them read; others to shield their eyes from the glaring screens and fluorescent lighting. Some appear flustered, others calm, though nothing very much in between. An occasional cry interrupts their busy work, as one of them solves a problem or wins a game they're playing.

"During the great floods—," explains Charlie, "the *Surge*—the Conqip adopted twenty-one kids on the Autism spectrum for their skills."

"Autism?" Nema asks, shaking her Spondylux.

Charlie frowns at Biermont and back at the bemused friends. "A hundred years ago, doctors noticed some children who had incredible focus and memory but struggled to cope with tasks other kids their age found simple. Like writing, opening a bottle top or tying their shoe laces; even just wearing their coat."

Nema wonders why the doctors found that so strange. *No one worries about stuff like that in RW. We learn things when we learn them; it's not a competition or race. Anyway, I wouldn't know where to start, putting on a coat. I needed help pulling on my PIE skin and using a knife till I was at least ten.*

Yes, my darling, yes you did, but you usually get there in the end. And as your dad always says, 'It doesn't matter either way, because there's always *your* way'.

Charlie continues, "The children also had trouble figuring out what other people said and what they meant. They often couldn't express what they wanted to say, and they lost friends because of it. Some called them loners, because they weren't bothered about being social and were happy spending time alone. That's where the word 'Autism' came from."

"The Greek word *eautos*?" pipes Nema. "It means 'self'." She wonders why being on your own was seen as bad; that's when she does her best, most creative work.

Izzy nudges her and smiles. "She means neurodivergent, doesn't she? Different thinkers—like us."

Charlie nods. "Quite. But before the Surge, autistics were

considered less able just because they were different. And they were given different labels depending on whether they spoke, how different they looked, how good they were at copying others to fit in. What it actually proved, though, was how well they hid their differences. It took another eighty years for the world to see how brilliant they really were, and by 2028, neurodivergents were leading the change toward a better world."

"So what's the deal with the Conqip?" asks Adam.

"There were people who feared the neurodivergents' ideas," explains Biermont. "They also disliked everyone being equal; it made them feel less important. Really, they were just afraid of having less stuff."

Charlie slips her hands in her pockets and steps over to Biermont. "The neurodivergents knew that the only way to make a better world was for people to start sharing and be their true selves again. But when the floods came more often, the Conqip—afraid they'd lose their luxuries—decided to build themselves a secret world. They enlisted the top autistic child coders in the country for their skills: these Auts, who designed and manage 'Gajoomdom'."

"So the SAs created the candy robots?" asks Nema.

"Indeed. The SAs were determined to please and do their best. The 'Gajoom' is their brain child."

Nema scans the withdrawn workers and gazes back at Biermont. *Have they been down here all this time? How did those horrible Conqip get away with it? How could those parents have let their children go?*

Sometimes, my love, we're just doing what we think is right. And sometimes, we just don't have the strength to do the right thing. You can't change the past, but you *can* change the future.

Charlie leads them through the rows of stations and now motionless workers. "This has become their life. They've been so focused in their work that they forgot the outside world."

Adam stalls behind Izzy to remember PIE story. "Why a race of sticks? And all this pure sugar...Wasn't it banned long before the Surge?"

"*Justement*, quite correct," pipes a familiar voice.

"Moojag!" calls Izzy.

The little guy leaps forward to greet them with a bow, realigning his hat and whisking back the gold letters. "Greedy Conqips," he whispers. "Whatever it takes to feed their sweet addiction."

"They built this new empire," explains Charlie, "to save

themselves from catastrophe, but most of all to keep living their selfish lives by their own rules."

Adam shakes his head. "But they'll only repeat PIE story all over—" Nema covers her ears from the buzz of the computers and Charlie's words, and turns her head from the light seeping through her mesh.

"So you've been down here since *then*?" Izzy asks. "And *no* one in RW has a clue?"

"Only Wats," says Charlie, "and now you three, of course."

"Morag?" asks Nema.

"There's very little that woman doesn't know."

But if Morag knew, what was the point in forcing me to stop thinking? Maybe all that was really just about the woman and 'our boy'…

"Eureeeeekaaaa!"

Charlie scans the room to a slouching Aut flinging his elastic arms about, as though drawing circles in the air. "This could be significant," she says, bee-lining for the gangly worker with Moojag teetering alongside her. "Hello, Sparky." The teen drops his arms and averts his gaze back at the screen. "Do you have something to share?" Charlie asks him. His eyes dart to the side, brows knitting in a frown.

"What she *means* is," says the girl bouncing on an inflatable ball beside him, "what have you *made* today, Sir

Sparky?" Her neat, silky plaits flap about as she rocks from side to side.

Charlie spots the confusion and rephrases her question. "Yes, Sparky, please do tell us what you have created."

The boy nods. Charlie nods back, waiting patiently for his response. He peers out the corner of his eye and whispers in his sister's ear. Sparkles leaps up, crossing her arms. "My brother says he's made a SUPER stick."

Charlie glances at Moojag. "I see. And what makes it so super?"

"What makes it so super?" repeats Sparkles in Charlie's exact tone.

Her brother turns his head without looking up and calls, "Replicated."

Charlie gasps as the hint of colour in her face drains away. "Self-replicating Gajooms?" Moojag hops back and glares round at Biermont. "It has already begun," says Charlie. "We must keep this from the Conqip as long as possible."

Sparky clamps his whirring head between his hands, as though it's set to explode. He gazes up at his sister and rubs his fist in a circle against his chest.

"Charlie," Sparkles sighs, "my brother says he is 'very sorry'."

15

CONQIP'S PLAN

Charlie reaches out to comfort Sparky, but he just shrinks away and shuffles back in his seat.

"It's okay; you've done nothing wrong. You're all just doing your job, and you're excellent at it. It's the Conqip's fault. They've been using your brains for their evil gain." Sparkles taps her brother's shoulder and returns to her station.

Nema, overhearing, shuffles up to Charlie. "But they're *already* multiplying," she whispers.

"It's true," adds Adam, joining them. "We saw it with our own eyes—those Gajooms who brought us here."

Sparkles huffs, gaping at her screen. "Couldn't have seen it with anyone *else's* eyes."

"Are you sure that's what you saw?" Charlie whispers, leaning into Adam.

Izzy presses a finger to her lips. "I'm not sure."

"That's 'cause you weren't there," whispers Adam.

"Right," adds Nema, "too busy scoffing sweets to even notice we'd gone."

Charlie turns to Biermont as Izzy combs her pouch for emergency toffees. "We need to work fast. It's possible Aldon already knows."

Sparky gazes up at the rectangular clock; it's almost the thirty-fourth hour. He always checks the time, for all the good it will do. The Conqip created new clocks, you see, adding more hours in the day to confuse the Auts and trick them into working longer. But with no access to sunlight, the Auts have lost track of real time anyway.

"It's time to uncover the Auticode," says Charlie, turning to Nema and her friends, "an antidote reversing any code that poses a threat to the Auts or the Gajooms."

Sparkles jumps off her ball and yanks at Charlie's jacket sleeve. "But it's locked in the Palace, and only the carer could have deciphered the code."

"And that's where you come in," whispers Charlie, looking round at Nema.

"But we don't know anything about antidotes."

Charlie smiles. "You're the *only* ones who can crack the code."

"*Oui,* special *whaikaha* you have," Moojag says, rubbing his velvety sleeve.

"Strengths," explains Charlie. "You come from the same generation of Auts. You also have knowledge that no one else has."

"Us?" asks Izzy.

"*Oui,*" Moojag answers. "Pattern, memory, logic, sensory—"

Charlie straightens Moojag's hat and smiles back at the friends. "The neurodivergents created the Real World, so they could finally live as their true selves and grow their unique abilities without fear."

"Before RW," adds Biermont, "autistics risked being ostracised for being too different."

Izzy smirks. "*Ostriches?*"

Nema slumps down on the ground to process the man's words. "It means bullied, Iz."

Adam peers through the mesh at the Auts absorbed in their work. "How come *we* didn't end up here too?"

"Wrong place, wrong time?" asks Izzy.

"*Right* place, *right* time, you mean," says Nema, shutting her eyes.

"You were too young to be chosen," explains Charlie. "And probably, like many pre-Surge Auts, you weren't diagnosed. Most girls were missed, because they hid their differences so well."

"Diagnosed?" asks Adam.

"Given a reason for your difference, for your difficulties," explains Biermont. Nema gazes suspiciously at Charlie. She doesn't remember ever having any 'difficulties'.

Charlie looks to Sparky. "There were many Auts who couldn't talk or simply chose not to," she explains. "Some just didn't see the point. Society considered them disabled because of it. I recognised their skills when no one else did; that's how they ended up here."

My girl wipes the tear from her cheek. *How could people be so cruel just because someone didn't talk or act like they did? Those bullies should've gotten the labels. When Spondylux finally wakes back up, I shall name them 'The Ignoramuses' and post it straight to PIE story.*

Charlie goes on, "When the Conqip discovered the Auts' unique abilities, they convinced their parents that the children were bad and that they were bad parents too. They persuaded them to hand over their children for a better life, where their skills would be put to 'good use'."

Moojag leaps forward, hands clasped. "Thirty-four-hour screen time and candy, perks of a sugar race creator."

"The Conqip found a way to get what they wanted," says

Biermont. "They no longer had to face their own faults or put up with natural living. They're free to eat junk until they literally puke."

"*Junk*?!" asks Adam. "And what's so bad about self-replicating sugar sticks?" Izzy swipes the caramel from her mouth and rubs her sore belly.

"Problem is," explains Charlie, "the Conqip are tiring of us all, of life underground with no natural light, of living on mostly artificial food. Stocks are running low, and we're all getting sicker."

"The Conqip leaders have been manipulating the innocent Auts," explains Biermont, "in breeding a Gajoom army to take over RW." The friends turn to each other and gulp. Nema tries to remember the last time anything like this happened. But there hasn't been any fighting or stealing, not since the 'Resource Wars' before the Surge.

"The Auts designed the Gajooms to be loyal, hard working and honest, like them," says Charlie, rocking her head. "But the code has been gradually modified to make them anxious, confused, and paranoid. Now they're in a constant state of 'fight or flight'. Who knows what they'll be capable of if we don't stop this now."

"They're very easily swayed," adds Moojag.

Izzy wobbles inside her disguise. "You can say that again."

"They're very easily swayed," repeats Sparkles, grinning.

Nema sticks herself to Izzy to haul them both back up. "What can we do to help?"

Charlie turns to Biermont. "I believe a Gajoom football match is getting underway. Can we make it over there in time?" Adam shakes his head; he's not a big football fan. Nema reckons it's just because he's not that good.

"Excellent idea," replies Biermont, "and Conqip III will be there for sure. He's their most prolific scorer. Never misses a game."

"Perfect, we'll steal the key off him during the match." Charlie turns to the friends. "The key unlocks the hiding place, in Pof Palace, of a magical book containing the special Auticode."

"Sure," Adam snorts, rolling his eyes at Nema. "Magical books, Gajooms playing football—"

"The Pofs aren't likely to betray the Conqip, though," Biermont reminds Charlie. "Not while they get all the sugar they want."

Charlie pats his sticky side. "Don't worry, Monty," she says, pulling a handkerchief from her pocket to wipe her hand clean. "We'll bribe our way in if we have to."

"HellOOooo," utters Sparkles. "Still here, you *know*."

"Would you like to come with us?"

Sparkles presses her sweaty palms together. "Where?"

"We're off to the match."

"But…what if someone asks me something; what will I say?"

"No one will ask you a thing."

"Ah, good job," she croaks. "And Sparky?"

"Sparky can come too, if he wants."

Izzy cocks her ear to some music pouring from the speaker and grabs her Spondylux.

Tra la la la la la, Tra la la la la la…

"It's The Wailers, Iz," says Nema.

"Wailing?" cries Sparkles. "Who's wailing?"

"Not *wailing*. The Wailers."

Sparkles rocks with relief. "Our favourite."

Sparky lurches behind her, singing, "*Soul captives are free…*"

Moojag jumps in, swaying to the left. "Bob Marley & The Wailers…The Best of the Wailers." He sways to the right. "Track four, two minutes, three seconds. Recorded 1969 to 1970. Released August 1971. *Not* a compilation."

Tra la la la la la…soul captives are free…

Nema watches the happy Auts, bobbing on their yoga balls and humming along. "It's their break," explains Charlie, spying the clock on the wall. "They're permitted to play a song of their choice."

Izzy chuckles. "They agree on one?"

Sparkles frowns, rolling back her shoulders and strumming her fingers to the beat. "We *all* love this one. Feels goooood...*looks* cool too." Nema wonders whether Sparkles is seeing purples and yellows, just like her.

You see, like me they see colours when they hear sounds. Nema's dad doesn't, but he does have his own thing with colours. Pre-Surgers called him 'colour blind', because he didn't see reds and greens like they did. At least they *thought* they all saw them the same. How could you ever be sure? In RW, others accept he just sees colours differently. Why wouldn't he? Surely *everyone* does...

"Just the one song?" asks Adam.

Biermont points to the clock. "They're allowed five minutes every thirty-four hours. They pick short tracks, that way they feel like they've listened to more."

Charlie points to a triangular opening at the opposite end of the lab and taps her ear. "We really must go."

Nema glances at the clock and back at the weary Auts. "Will there be honey cake?" asks Izzy, swivelling round.

Adam smirks. "I'm sure we'll find you something in this land of confectionery."

"Gajooms make delicious brownies." Izzy's pout turns to

a freakish grin. "But," Charlie adds, raising a brow as Izzy flumps with a broken sigh, "I'm afraid you're going to have to work for it."

"We're playing football," groans Adam.

"No choice; you're too obvious otherwise," says Charlie. "Anyway, we need to snatch the key off the Conqip at the game."

Sparkles eyes the clock. "Conqip approaching," she says, grating her forehead with a jagged nail, "in ten point five seconds."

"Right," Charlie calls, marching passed the jittery Auts, "follow *me*. The Conqip will be here any moment on their rounds."

Sparkles shoos her brother back to his station. "We'd better stay and work." Sparky mumbles to himself, skipping off to the tune as it fades out.

Tra la la la la la, Tra la la...

Charlie darts through the opening, followed by the others as the next track cues in.

"Is that Soul Captives, again?" Adam asks Biermont.

"Sure is. Must've heard it a thousand times."

16

GAJOOM vs CONQIP

"*Ouch…*"

Charlie glances back. "Watch your heads. The walls are sixty-degree-angled."

"Icicles triangle?" Izzy calls.

"Isosceles," says Nema.

"Equilateral," Adam calls back. "If all sides and angles are equal then—"

"You're quite right," declares Moojag, darting between them. "However, *gaijins*, you are travelling through an open-ended Triangular Prism. Polyhedron of triangular base…" he mutters, hovering on ahead. "Translated copy, three faces adjoining corresponding sides."

Adam moves in from the narrowing walls. Nema and Izzy stumble into line behind him as the distant hum of overworked computers fades away.

Nema glances back. "What about Sparkles and Sparky?"

"SAs need time to get used to new things!" hollers Moojag, before vanishing with Charlie and Biermont.

Nema slams into Adam, and finds herself sandwiched between him and Izzy. "Dead end."

"No, it's not," says Adam calmly.

"Turn back!" cries Nema.

Izzy whimpers, attempting to prise her velcro-like self from my girl. "It's dark, I can't—"

"Down here…" echoes the faint voice of Biermont.

Adam probes the wall in front of them with both hands. "Okay, it's just a really tight bend."

Nema and Izzy giggle.

Adam hasn't a clue what those two are imagining up this time. "Maybe you should go first," he says, rolling his eyes at them chuckling away. "Stay if you like, I'm outta here."

"No, wait!" calls Nema, shuffling along.

"Crouch," calls Adam. "The ceiling just got lower."

"Crouch," sniggers Nema.

"I know," says Izzy as Adam speeds up. "Good job it's dark," she whispers. "Bet we look ridonculous."

"Speak for yourself," splutters Nema.

"There's light ahead," Adam calls back.

Nema wheezes, forced into a caterpillar crawl, as an eerie

sound seeps into the sunken passage. Izzy stops to listen to the mashed-up chanting and a whistle blowing. Nema folds her arms up to cover her ears and hisses at her friend rummaging her pouch like a squirrel.

Izzy gulps down a lemon drop. "What?"

"*Now?*"

"For my ears!" Izzy cocks her head to the sound of cheering.

"Adam's gone," says Nema.

"Where?"

"It's the end, Izzy!"

"You're *soooo* dramatic."

Nema wiggles out the tunnel and unfurls her body, just as Adam is whisked away by two colossal Gajooms. She squirms back, but another pair sweep in and attach themselves to her sides. They bound off, with her dangling between them, into the glare of the flood-lit stadium.

Izzy pokes her head out and freezes as more candy-stick robots dive in to seize her, too. They drag her into the air and bolt hastily across the pitch with her desperately clinging onto the inside of her disguise. The Gajooms plunge Nema and Adam down, pulling in opposite directions to draw themselves from the dizzy friends.

The crowd-filled stadium buzzes louder and harder than at

Stikleby Hall. The stands filled with drunken Gajoomdomers. Above them, in a VIP tier behind two screens that bulge out like bug eyes, are cheering over-fed Conqip men accompanied by their squawking Pofs.

Adam unwinds his twisted Gajoom suit, peels his feet from the sticky turf, and gajumps over to Nema. "Lost Iz, again," he whispers.

"She's over there, in goal. See? The one with candies stuck to her butt." *DO Gajooms have bums though?* Nema wonders. *They're the same all the way round, surely...*

I wouldn't put it past them, my love.

Nema watches Izzy bend down awkwardly in her stripy suit to admire a glittering gold ball, before an agile Gajoom twice her height bounds in and nudges it away. The stick jumps back before leaping forward and belting the gleaming ball across the pitch. It flies right over them and drops to the ground, before miraculously rolling back on itself into the centre.

"Er, this'll be interesting," says Adam.

"You'll be fine."

"Yes, he will," pipes Biermont.

The still unfamiliar voice makes Nema jump. "But how'll

we *kick* without a *foot*?" she asks.

"Just leap in and lob."

"Mono-football?" grumbles Adam, lagging behind. "I guess you wouldn't use both your feet anyway. Would you?"

It helps, thinks Nema, dodging a wispy, pink candy cloud. It floats up and drifts past two huge blue and white striped banners. Dozens of Pofs hover around the pitch to the rhythm of the anthoom. They dart in and out of the Conqip and Gajoom players, conjuring more distracting candy clouds.

"Where are the Auts?" calls Adam, through the crowd's raucous cheers.

"Can't handle the sounds, nor the smell," explains Biermont. "They'll be watching from the lab."

"Smell?" asks Nema.

"Whenever the Conqip score, a potent whiff of aged cheese—usually Stilton—gets pumped over the opposing team's end of the pitch."

"What if the other team scores?"

"Another pump."

"On the Conqip?"

"What? Of course not, no. On the Gajooms again."

"Not fair."

"Matches are never fair," Charlie sighs, appearing from nowhere. "'Fair' was the first word erased from the old

English dictionary."

"So we'll lose, whatever happens," says Adam.

"You *could* win, but *please* don't do that."

"Why *not*?" pipes Izzy, sneaking up on them.

Nema notices the crowd begin to settle. "Of course not," she whispers. "They'll totally suss."

Charlie nods.

"Aren't we drawing attention to ourselves?" asks Adam.

"All thirty-four Gajooms must play; it's law. If you don't, you'll stand out like a sore thumb."

"We won't, because we're purple and white," mutters Nema. She scans the crowd-filled stand. Meaty men jeering, little winged girls shimmying by their side. Charlie heads over to the stands, waves to a tall older man in the glass-fronted tier, and turns to face the pitch as Kitty Poof zooms through the stadium. She flies to and fro, like a yoyo, between big bites of her rainbow-iced doughnut.

"You have to grab the key before the game's up," says Biermont.

"Which one?" whispers Nema, scanning the sneery-faced Conqip players in their tight, blue and white stripy kit.

"Player III, one of the attackers."

"The one at the front then?" asks Adam.

Nema leans into the ex-Conqip and whispers, "He doesn't

do football—"

"Only gotta kick it in the goal, right?" asks Adam.

Nema shakes her head, crossing her fingers under the Gajoom suit. *Poor Adam. He hasn't a clue, which would be just fine if he wasn't a stick of rock in the middle of a pitch about to get slaughtered by a bunch of nasty pre-Surge bullies. They do look mean, but how much damage could they really do?*

Their words can play tricks on your mind, my love, for a very long time.

Biermont pokes Adam. "Just try to look like you know what you're doing. Player III has the grey tuft of hair brushed up from his forehead. The key will be clipped to his shorts. When the game's up, we'll meet over at the benches."

Nema whispers bye to Biermont, as everyone bounds across the pitch. She's never seen so many players in a game. The jeering finally lets up with a Pof hovering out of a round hole in the VIP box. Nema recognises the cat-eye glasses and sherbet-striped scarf as Poof Poof swoops into centre circle and hovers between Gajoom 21 and Conqip II. The curvy Pof leader curtseys and blows a big red candy-whistle, declaring the match underway.

Conqip II—a poised, broad-shouldered man in his thirties with frizzy, grey hair and coarse stubble—jogs in and hogs the ball from G21. "Where has bloody IV bummed off to this time?" the Conqip hollers at number VI, shortest of the Conqip, bald and pale.

The sour-faced player hunches his shoulders and dashes in for the ball as Conqip II passes, but G21 spins into its path diverting it to Adam. Adam bravely bounds straight in but misses it by an inch.

"He's got the strength and the pace," observes the capped commentator, "athletic too. Just lacks the natural touch of a footballer…"

Well, of course not, thinks Nema. *He's a Gajoom, isn't he. Well, okay, he's not.* My girl spots her chance. She takes a giant leap forward for the ball, but cheating Conqip II juts out an arm and sends her soaring.

"What's this?" booms the livid commentator. The rioting, heaving crowd glare at her hurtling straight for Conqip III. "Can you bloody believe it? A dopey Gajoom diving in for a Conqip!" He throws his arms up as Nema smashes into the man's large flailing body, burying his face in the ground.

Poof Poof swoops in at once, chomping on her whistle as she waves a giant yellow card over the deflated Gajoom. Nema freezes, splayed over the man fitting the key-holder's description. Just able to see through her mesh hole, she checks over his kit and spots a small key dangling from his overstretched waistband.

No hands! How on earth do they expect me to get a key off the guy without my hands?

As the flattened Conqip jerks his arm out from under her to fix his feeble quiff, she tries poking her pinky through the spy mesh. But the holes are too small. In fact, there *aren't* any holes.

"Get off," groans the man."Get off me PDQ" (pretty damn quick) "you moronic creature!" Nema bolts up, chest beating along with her pulsating PIE.

"RED CARD that defunct, evil piece of..." she hears a smug Conqip yell in the stands as Poof Poof dives in to shoo her off the pitch.

Nema shuffles over to the bench and slumps down with the growing line-up of deflated Gajooms. *Who are these grim Conqips?* she thinks. *What must have happened to make them so very mean?* She edges round to spy the VIP box. A suited old man is peering down through the glass, yelling something with his fists in the air. She imagines he's chanting 'Come on, you Conqips!' like the people in the stands. A red-haired Pof, waiting eagerly at his side, gapes cloudy-eyed at his bulging candy-filled pockets. He glances at the bench where Nema sits, shouts at the Conqip behind him, then grabs the Pof by her long hair and charges out, pulling her after him.

Nema strokes the back of her head. It hurts, as though her own hair has just been yanked. *How did that poor Pof not even flinch?* She turns back round to look at the sticks beside her, slouched over like pre-Surge humans. *I know they're only robots, but they seem to communicate and have emotions too. Maybe their skin works like PIE, and that's how they know what to feel. They sure SMELL human...* Nema twitches her nose at a strong whiff filling her nostrils *...like pre-Surge, stinky feet.*

The crowd roars, making her jump, as half the remaining Gajooms hurdle off the pitch followed by a stinking tornado of rotting cheese. "And off the pitch they go," splutters the commentator. He presses his eyes closed, releasing his wet lips from the slimy mic as he lurches back in his booth. "With a measly few Gajooms remaining, an inevitable WIN for *us* hangs in the balance."

"Out of the way!" Poof Poof orders the Gajooms, herding them to give the enraged Conqip a clear pass.

"Gajooms' gotta bolt," the commentator bellows into his mic. "Get in there, Conqips..." Poof Poof waves on an extra Conqip player with her wand, dribbling a little spit as she blows her dwindling whistle.

"In toward honourable number III...Now in possession of the ball...What does he do with NO Gajoom in sight?..." The commentator hollers over the throbbing crowd now chanting the anthoom. "Not much chance for the Gajooms... and...oh, YES! Here it comes, and IN IT GOES. There it is—VICTORY! Conqip III scores the deciding goal."

Nema glances back up at the empty VIP box before bolting off the pitch after Charlie as the crowd filters out of the stadium.

"It's over when the lazy Conqip say it is," whispers Biermont, leaping over to Izzy who's staring up at the clock.

"The key?"

"Nope."

Izzy wipes her sweaty brow and sighs, fiddling with her Spondylux. "Home?"

"Not quite," says Biermont, giving her a gentle shove in the direction of Charlie and the others. "Time to get the Gajooms back to work and track down that special little book."

17

THE SWEET DELIVERY

Charlie waves the Gajooms into a long 'changing room'. "Mustn't dilly dally, Aldon will be furious and headed straight for the factory."

"But they *won*," says Nema.

"You took down a Conqip. That's never ever happened before."

Nema slumps her weary body and shakes her head. "It's not *my* fault I got Conqip tripped?"

"*They* won't see it that way," says Charlie. "It's done; there's nothing we can do."

Izzy stamps her foot. "*Nothing*?"

"Just stay quiet, and let us take the lead," whispers Biermont.

It's easy staying quiet, thinks Nema, *but when someone's telling you NOT to speak—that's a lot harder to do.*

"Sure," whispers Adam, nudging his friends, "we won't say a word, *will* we?" Nema raises a brow and clamps her mouth closed.

"We're going up to the factory," says Charlie, directing the line of jittery sticks across the dimly-lit room. "It's where the Gajooms make our sweets."

Biermont points to the launchpad in the corner and a clear shaft above it that stretches right up through the ceiling. Izzy gulps a mint and leaps into line behind him as the last Gajooms shoot up the tube. They watch, brows raised, as the robots fly up and out through the ceiling.

"If we don't get them back to work right away, the Conqip will have us crushed like rejected candy," says Charlie, shoving the last wavering Gajoom onto the launchpad. Izzy swivels round, choking on her own saliva. "The Conqip have lost their way, I'm afraid they'll never change."

"I saw one drag a Pof by her hair," whispers Nema. Charlie shakes her head. "Another one called me evil and—"

"Well, we won't have to put up with them for much longer," says Biermont. "But first the Conqips' sweets need delivering—our next chance to get that key."

"See you up there," Charlie calls, slipping inside the column.

Izzy and Nema giggle at the woman's hair standing on

end as a blast of air shuttles her to the middle of the tube before shooting her up through the ceiling. Adam edges Izzy forward. "Go on, you two next. Ga-jump." The girls wiggle onto the pad and hover off the ground. Adam waits for them to rocket and leaps on last with Biermont.

***

Charlie heads for the far side of the long factory as the others slide head first into the sweet-smelling room: vanilla, caramel, lime, strawberry, peppermint...

It's literally the inside of a mammoth, hollowed-out candy stick. The Gajooms, in their positions either side of an assembly line, are already working up a candy sweat. Sugar and flavour loaders at one end of the rotating belt, quality controllers crammed into the middle, and packers offloading confectionery at the other end.

Charlie nudges some stray Gajooms over to the sorting section. She signals to a pile of candy on the floor, rejected for their various imperfections. They pounce forward and pound the discarded sweets. The sugar encrusted floor crunches with each strike before a pummelled mass is finally swept into a giant pit.

"Hurry," calls Biermont. A pink light flashes above the factory door, and a rusty old speaker jutting from the wall blares out the anthoom.

Adam hisses to Nema as a door into the factory inches open. But she's locked in thought. Standing alone in the centre of the room, she gazes at the Gajooms hunched over the conveyor. *No wonder they slouch, schlepping away in that position all day—*

"BRAVO, bravo," jeers an old man in a flecked grey suit. Aldon, Conqip's founder, strides into the room. The stern unforgiving stare complements his receding hair line. He tucks his walking stick under his arm and claps. The Gajooms stop still as he lurches with a limp across the factory floor, trailed by his two deputies. "YOU there!" He sneers, craning his neck and scrunching up his nose at the suspiciously short Gajoom in his way. "What on earth is the matter with you, blockhead?"

"Yes, you! THICK stick," says Brix, Conqip's number II. Nema trembles under the disguise along with her vibrating skin. "Have you forgotten that misbehaviour results in a fatal candy CRUSHING?"

Nothing is budging this Gajoom, though, and nothing infuriates the Conqip more. Aldon's face swells as it reddens. "This malformity of a Gajoom is all your fault," he says, turning to Travis, Conqip III.

"Oh, *that* old chestnut?" grunts the stubbled man, flicking back his drooping quiff. "Don't point the finger at me again."

Aldon fumes. "I *cannot* be expected to take care of everything. The hostility gene was your idea, was it not?"

"Oh, how convenient, turning it round to suit you…"

Nema gawks through the mesh at the Conqip's hardened faces. *What did chestnuts ever do to them? Maybe they don't like nuts?*

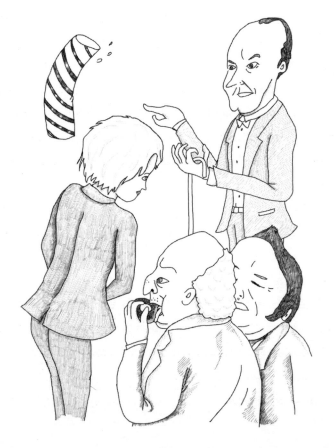

Brix growls at Travis and turns to Aldon, arms crossed. "Isn't it about time he did some *real* work around here, A?"

"What's that supposed to mean?" asks Travis.

"Your taste for sugar," says Brix, sticking his nose in the air. "Quite frankly, it's just tasteless."

Travis jolts his head back, throwing up his arms. "Tasteless? You're a fine one to talk."

"I like a sweet as much as the next," scoffs Brix, "but at least I can control myself."

"I don't have a sugar problem," says Travis.

"Hmmm, sure about that, are we?"

"Deny it all you like, number two, but it's *you* who seriously needs help."

Brix grunts. "My sugar intake is my business, nobody else's."

"It's no wonder they all abandoned you."

Brix huffs. "No one left *me;* I left *them*. Who in their right mind wants to live in a miserly 'natural' world, 'sharing' things? *Ughhh*."

"Kid yourself all you like. You alienate everyone, and you're just too into yourself to accept the plain truth."

"Get lost," says Brix, grabbing a fat ring doughnut from the belt. He shamelessly gobbles a huge chunk right in Conqip III's haggard face.

Travis hops back. "That's right, bury your head in the sugar, as usual."

"I *will*."

Travis reaches for the conveyor belt behind him to sneak a cherry tart. "Hypocrite," he whispers, dropping it into his blazer pocket and storming off.

Aldon sneers, turning back from his squabbling minions with a raised, ragged brow. "Will you stick there *all* day? Or do we cram you in the crusher?" Biermont leaps over, bumping into Nema to stick himself to her and whisk them back over to the Gajooms.

"Finally the idiot gets it," says Travis.

"What do you expect?" says Brix. "It's only a stick of bloody rock."

"Did no such thing," says Aldon. "G21 saved its bacon. Charlie, hurry them up and bring us our tasting selection. These deviations are quite unsatisfactory."

Charlie bows and signals the Gajooms back to work. "I do apologise, A, sincerely. Rest assured, the ritziest of candies will be delivered for your evaluation within the hour."

"Make it half, and don't very well be late or *you* know what."

"Of course, A."

Brix sniggers, ogling the awkward looking candy robots.

"Those Auts *OUGHT* to do better."

"If you ask *me*," says Travis, "the Gajooms are looking a tad weaker, not fiercer."

Aldon scans the busy robots. "Just keep your eye on that G21, Charlie. It's getting much too conscious for my liking."

"Hear, hear!" calls Travis, mirroring Brix's swishy hips as they make for the door.

"CHARLIE," yells Aldon, without looking back.

"Yes, A?"

"The THICK stick who caused the scene: that one to deliver our sweets. *Not* bacon-saving G21. CLEAR?"

"Of course," replies Charlie, frowning at Biermont. "No problem."

"No problem," sniggers Travis.

"Of course, A…No problem, A," sniggers Brix.

"I could murder a juicy woodpecker," whispers Travis, drooling. "The other Conqips better not have started without us."

Brix pats his beefy belly. "*Ooooh*, that time already?"

"Always brunch time," says Aldon as they march out for Conqip Hall.

***

Charlie heads straight to the sticky production line. "We've got to impress, to keep the tyrants sweet. What have you for me today?"

Gajoom number six, heading the assembly, arches over the belt and attaches its upper half to a foot-wide, gold-leaf-laced chocolate peanut butter cup. It rotates with a jumbo ga-jiggle and shakes off the massive sweet into a nearby cart. "Good choice, G6."

Encouraged, it returns to load another. The rest follow, leaping in and gathering up the biggest, sweetest, most luscious candy to present the Conqip. From mammoth, marshmallowy nougat bars to oozing, two-foot-long chocolate fudge brownies and oversized rhubarb and custard bonbons, almost any sweet you could imagine is hatching in this sticky factory.

Izzy's mouth waters at an even more extraordinary sight. "3D-printed sweets!" she cries, nudging her friends.

"What?" says Nema, still thinking of her ill-fated woodpecker friend, Bill.

Adam ogles the giant peanut butter cups cruising the belt as Izzy bounds through a cocoa breeze to a parallel production line. She clasps her hands at a breathtaking neon-latticed candy cage. "Can we try a bit?"

Charlie nods, grabbing a glowing multi-sided geometric sour and snapping her off a section.

"Icosahedron," says Nema, finally joining them.

"It's a bonbon, not a *dinosaur*," Izzy spurts, savouring the tang of the delicate apple'n'lime construction.

"Its *shape*, Iz. It has twenty sides."

"Vacuus," says Adam, casually propped against the curved candy wall like a leaning statue.

"*Absolument* correct," sparks Moojag, reappearing from nowhere again and poking Adam in his middle. "A perfect hollowed icosahedron."

The Gajoom in charge of 3D sweets twerks to the beat of the anthoom. It deposits the last lattice into the cart and shuffles along the belt to attach itself to an enormous orange gummy bear. The crystal-encrusted sweet is almost the Gajoom's size in height but a great deal wider.

Nema's jaw drops at the wobbling giant and the Gajoom toppling from its weight. *How could anyone even think about eating a life-sized bear made of pure sugar?*

"This is quite sufficient to satisfy the Conqip," says Charlie. "Knocking them out just long enough to recover the key and make for the palace."

Moojag waves his hat in the air, hovering between the Gajooms and chanting, "*Splendide sélection! Plus enticement, plus addictive!* Putty in your hands. And the *lattice de pomme*," he whispers, spinning round on one leg, "—genius choice for our sour-faced leader."

The Gajooms have filled the carts mountain-high with confectionery and are preparing to wedge themselves between the handle bars.

"Hold it," Charlie calls to them. "Our *new* Gajooms will be taking care of the delivery today." She turns to the Real World friends. "Aldon specifically requested Nema deliver the sweets, so I'm afraid you three must go this one alone."

Nema gazes at Biermont as activity in the factory comes to a stand still.

"Monty has already risked himself saving you today, and they demanded he not go. I simply won't chance him being recognised."

"We can do this," says Adam, with Izzy shifting away and the Gajooms returning to work.

Charlie winks at Izzy. "I know we can count on you, too. Your friends could do with your support."

"So, all we have to do," asks Nema, "is deliver these weird sweets, right?"

"And acquire the key from Conqip III," adds Biermont.

"Come on Izzy," says Adam, "don't make us do this on our own."

"Okay…" she says, licking her acidic, sugary lips and sucking the lattice fragment on her tongue, "but I'm delivering the 3D things—and I'm *not* getting the key."

"It'll only take a minute," explains Biermont. "They'll polish off the sweets and get wired from the sugar rush. You'll have the pleasure of watching them pass out like a light."

"At which point," Charlie continues, "you can sneak in and snatch the key from Travis."

Izzy wipes her clammy palms down the inside of the Gajoom skin. "Then what?" asks Nema.

"We'll be waiting for you, right here. Don't worry."

'Don't worry'?—How are they so cool about it? And as for passing out like a light, we could be waiting a while. The sun takes at least an hour to fully set; even then, it's not completely dark. Solar lights take an age to go out too.

Adam boldly bounces up to the overflowing peanut-butter cup cart and glances back at Charlie.

"You can't miss it," she says. "Out this door and straight down the sloping hallway. You'll find them behind the double doors."

Nema shuffles up to the cart suffering the colossal gummy bear, its middle bulging shamelessly over the sides. She wedges herself between the handlebars and jolts it forward. Izzy clings to the 3D-candy cart and takes off after her friends through the open factory door.

Ga-joooom…STIK! Ga-joooom…STIK! Ga-joooom…

18

CANDY BRUNCH

…*STIK!*

"I smell Gajoom," sneers a stuffed Brix. He lies back on his double-decker chaise longue; the stem of a champagne flute teeters between his pinched fingers.

Aldon paces the hall, hands clasped behind his back. "For goodness' sake, what has taken them so long?"

"You're consuming rather a lot lately, A?" says Travis, grinning.

Aldon looks him up and down. "Concern yourself with your own dietary habits."

"I'll have you know," says Travis, "I'm in fantastic health."

Brix snickers. "Your fantastic pair of man boobs is proof of that."

Aldon sneers at his men. "Ludicrous. Why must you buffoons always be so vulgar."

"Hypocrite," Brix hisses under his breath.

"I *beg* your pardon?"

"Nothing at all."

"Why don't you get off your fancy high-chair and attend to the door?"

"*I'll* do it," says Travis, already turning the knobs and letting the heavy wooden doors swing wide open. "It's a hulking great studded BEAR."

"WHAT? I'll have that Charlie's head," Aldon says. Nema quickly shuffles out from behind the bear as he charges for the door with Brix.

"What witchcraft is this?" scoffs Brix, inspecting the Godzilla of a gummy.

Aldon stretches off its left arm, "Apparently, a ginormous jewelled gum sweet," and cautiously bites into it.

Brix gawks at him. "Good?"

"Not my thing."

Travis grumbles, plucking off the biggest crystal. "What *is* your thing, A?"

"A less flexible sweet. One that doesn't take forever to chew or pull out one's remaining teeth...*Well* Gajooms? Don't just *STIK* there in the doorway; bring in the monster and the rest of your weird oversized concoctions."

Ga-joooom...STIK, Ga-joooom...STIK, Ga-joooom...

STIK bound the uneasy three into the hall. Brix directs them past portraits of men in pre-Surge dinner suits and a row of stuffed animals' heads jutting from the wall. Travis slouches over the banquet table, tutting impatiently as the fake Gajooms park the carts up alongside it. Nema gawks at Aldon, swiping his arm across the filthy table. He shifts the strewn pewter dishes of leftover food to clear a space.

She imagines all the greedy men around the table earlier, wolfing down the food. She barely recognises the remains, not because they're half-eaten, but, because she's never seen most of this stuff before. A butchered poached sole, a single limp shrimp, a silver bowl of scarcely touched caviar, and a trail of frail dismantled skeletons flung unapologetically over an ornate tray. One dish stands out from the rest that makes her want to retch: a tousled tower of cracked blue shells and a pile of red-tipped claws.

"Wait over there!" demands Aldon, pointing to the door.

"Yes, dumbos, don't hawk like that," says Brix, scoffing a giant peanut butter cup and licking the chocolate-coated infected sore at the corner of his mouth. "Show some respect."

Nema and her friends turn gladly for the door. She pictures the unthinking people of the old world, hiding in their stuffy houses with no care for the future. *How could they not have shared their food and water? Hoarding all their stuff like that. At least now there's no more fighting, and we have enough food to eat. But that could all change. What if we can't stop the Conqip? What'll happen to the Real World if we fail?*

Trust your intuition, my love, and everything will be all right.

The Conqip raid the carts, barely breathing between bites. Permanent grins on their pasty faces.

"She *has* done well," remarks Brix.

"Indeed, a fine choice."

Brix inspects the candy's delicate geometry. "This must be the new 3D fare? We really are down with the kids."

"Down?" asks Aldon. "This product is rightfully ours, not some worthless kids'."

"Err, one might say, 'acquired'," Travis splutters, licking the new tech candy, "but yeah, sure."

"How very DARE you—"

"I thought…the tech came from 'upstairs'?"

"You *thought*, you *thought*…"

Brix and Travis jolt back as Aldon lines up three icosahedrons on the table. Seizing a gold carving knife, he stabs each cage wildly in succession. Multicoloured shards fly in every direction.

Upstairs? wonders Nema. *They must mean RW.*

Izzy quivers at the same thought. "They nicked our tech," she whispers as Adam and Nema bump her at once.

Brix cocks his head. "What was that?"

"Hearing things again?" says Travis, kicking his feet up.

"Shut up, shut up!" hollers Brix, clambering onto the table and cupping a hand to his ear.

Aldon leans forward in his grand armchair, crossing his arms over his legs. "How many times have I told you about extremities on the table."

"Live a little, A!" shouts Brix.

Travis' eyes go skew and, sure enough, his head drops, sinking face first into the gummy bear's tummy. Brix glares at him disapprovingly before collapsing too into a heap on the table. Aldon flops back in his chair, letting his arms fling down. He snorts like a pig and, with a jolt, nods off to sleep.

"Quick," Adam whispers to Nema, "get the silly costume off, so you can grab the key."

She tips herself onto the floor, squirms out of the tube, and crawls over to Travis. Izzy grits her teeth and clasps her hands. With the Conqip's arms conveniently wrapped round the bear's middle, Nema reaches into his jacket pocket. She feels around the sticky rubble of a crushed tart and turns to her friends, shoulders hunched. She creeps round the Conqip to dip her hand in his other pocket...

CREAAAAAK!

"The door," hisses Adam. "No—the *other* one."

Nema hesitates as a door at the opposite end of the hall edges open and Poof Poof darts in.

"Mum," cries Kitty, following right behind her.

"Darling, you must trim those wings of yours," Poof screeches, almost rousing the Conqip. "Deary me, such utter chaos in here."

"Mummy!"

"Can't you see I'm busy!"

"Gajooms."

Poof Poof swerves, peers down, and lunges at the sticks. "What's this? G9? Or is it 8? Maybe 4? Something a little different about you this day, Gajoom." She squints through her edgy little specs at Nema, all rumpled from hurriedly slipping back into her disguise. "Wouldn't you agree, Kitty?"

Kitty hovers by her side, cackling and shaking her finger.

"*Yes.* Mummy *always* right."

Nema quickly realigns her tube while Poof Poof isn't looking and shimmies back over to the others. Kitty zooms up and down the cluttered table, shaking her head. "No cake."

Poof Poof dives round the carts and stalls over the 3D sweets. "What is this nonsense?" She hoists an icosahedron with her wand. "Here, especially for you, darling."

"Thank you, mummy." Kitty accepts the unfamiliar latticed object, carefully inspects it, and nibbles on an apple-flavoured triangular side.

"Well done, Gajooms," declares Poof Poof, seeing her daughter's face light up. "Most impressive, don't you think, darling?" Kitty nods, face puckering from the sour twang. "Well, for what do you await, Gajooms? Chop, chop!"

Nema and her friends leap out the hall, leaving Poof Poof mumbling and shaking her wand over the Conqip.

"Senseless men," grumbles the Pof, chomping on a peanut butter cup. "Using the feeble, feather-brained Auts when there are so many talented Pofs." She retrieves a tiny object before whizzing out the door she entered.

"Mummy?" calls Kitty, tailing after.

"Yes, sausage."

"What's that key for?"

19

OUT OF JUICE

Adam bounds into the factory first, stumbling into Charlie and Moojag. "Poof Poof's onto us—"

"What happened?" asks Charlie.

"I tried," says Nema, stalling to rub her hot, itchy face. "Poof Poof came in, and Kitty saw me."

"She may have figured out what we're up to," says Charlie, "and gone in there for the key too. We must get to Pof Palace."

Moojag hovers round them. "*Gaijins*, follow me."

Izzy flops down. "We could really do with a charge," she groans.

"We need sun," says Nema. "We stopped getting alerts hours ago."

Charlie looks at Adam laying on the ground and kneels down beside him. "How are you doing, my friend?"

"I think..." he answers meekly.

"Without sun," explains Nema, "our PIEs just aren't functioning how they're meant to. We're losing track of what we need to stay healthy, the time too."

"Biermont, we should get them to Porto Gajoom right away."

"No go. No time."

"We can't have our visitors passing out on us—"

"How about MT? I know it's just D2 with added D3, but it might do the trick?"

"Good, yes, that should keep them going. They're not used to being underground, let alone indoors. Without sun, their vitamin D levels will be low. But natural light, I'm afraid, will have to wait for now."

Nema flails to the ground beside Adam. "Please…just a bit of time to—"

"Friends, rest a while. Then we'll get you what you need. But we *must* get to the Palace to retrieve the key and that book before Poof Poof gets her hands on it."

"No *problème*." Moojag grabs a massive brownie off a Gajoom, grips the letters of his hat with his other hand and spins on his heels. "I will retrieve said key." The room darkens, and a dazzling green light flashes as he vanishes without a trace.

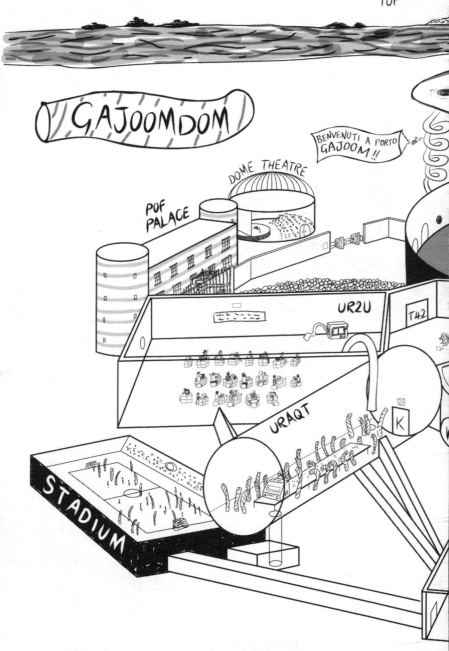

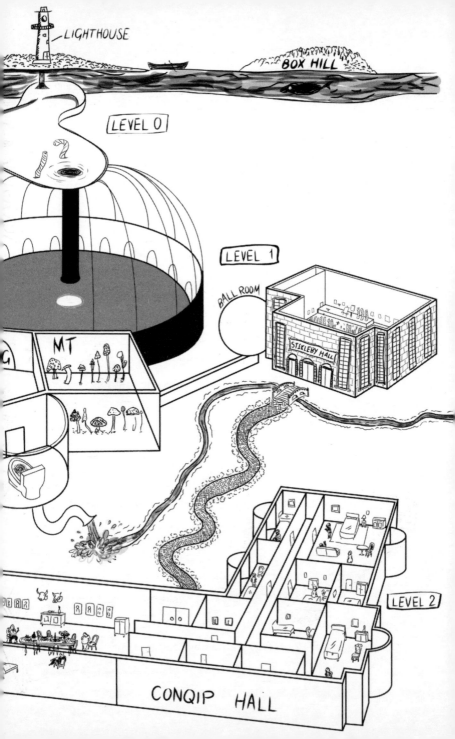

20

MOOJAG AND THE KEY

Poof Poof nudges her daughter into the switching room. "Kitty, you sit here and enjoy the rest of your sweet."

"Dorothy?"

"Of course, darling, watch anything you like."

"Witch is dead," Kitty chants, crossing her chunky, little legs in front of her.

Poof Poof zooms back for the door. "Yes, darling, whatever you want; I'm busy now, very busy."

"Early dinner…" Kitty mutters to herself before calling the words louder, but her mum has already gone. She dons her headphones, sets the volume full blast, and presses play on the screen.

Moojag pops his head into the room and Kitty taps pause with her long-nailed finger. "WHAT?" she asks, crossing her arms and squinting up at him. "Busy now."

"I need Poof Poof. Did you see where she went?"

"Busy now." Kitty's finger hovers over the play icon as Moojag steps forward, proffering a very, *very* large sagging fudge brownie. Her jaw drops and she drools, holding out her arms like a zombie.

"For you, *ma petite saucisse.*" She giggles, sniffing the cake as Moojag balances it over her outstretched arms. "Poof Poof went *which* way now?"

"*Witch?*" says Kitty, grinning through a mouthful of chocolatey goo. Poised to un-pause the video, she cradles the brownie in one arm and, without looking up, points to door T42.

Moojag salutes her and zooms out into the grounds of Pof Palace, home to Poof Poof and the Pofs. The landscape is purple, and the phoney sky ceiling is covered in dark purple patches. Crystallised clouds of pink candy floss that has floated up and stuck to it over time. Moojag hovers across a winding path of peach marshmallow pebbles, to the entrance of the blue and white striped building before him.

He spots Poof Poof slipping through the ornate golden gate with its playful cherubs and two-headed eagle at the top. She swerves, clutching the heavy ring of keys swinging by her side, and squints back at Moojag. "WHAT, *Aut?*"

"I need to discuss with you—cake."

Poof Poof throws her arms in the air, tilting with the

weight of the keys dangling from her belt. "*Which* cake?"

Moojag clasps his hands. "For Kitty. She has asked the Auts for a birthday cake. I should request your formidable *conseil*."

She glares at him with pursed lips. She can't bear it when anyone else speaks a foreign language. Especially when she hasn't got a clue what they're saying.

"Your good advice?"

"Of course, my darling," she replies, steering into the palace. "*Vite, vite* though. I'm *très* busy you know."

Moojag passes by the gates and follows her in through the double, wooden doors. Poof Poof grins, plopping herself onto a tall throne covered in rich, purple velvet. It's covered in satisfyingly symmetrical patterns of intertwined flowers, oak leaves, and yet more chubby angels. Moojag leans against the side of the chair right by her bunch of keys.

"Cake, you say?"

"*Oui.*"

Poof Poof taps her chin and squints up at the glistening pendants hanging from the chandelier. "I suggest rich chocolate, triple-layered, completely covered in pink frosting—of course—and finished with eighteen diamonds. But MOIST," she adds, smacking her lips, "it *has* to be *moist.*"

Moojag raises a brow and gazes down at the jangling keys bulging through the chair's arm. "*Bien sûr*, of course." His mind wanders as he dreams up a cake of his own. A simple jam-filled sponge, lightly dusted with icing sugar, just like the one his grandmother used to bake for him. You see, it was his birthday yesterday, but he wasn't allowed a cake. '*You don't deserve birthday cake*,' is what mean Aldon and the others always tell him and the Pofs, '*because you idiots never bloody grow up!*'

"They must be *real* jewels," continues Poof Poof. "My sausage will know."

"*Bien sûr,*" says Moojag. He looks away, rolling his eyes, and spots the tiny gold key dangling on an individual key chain. He lowers his arm while Poof Poof, distracted by the shimmying pendants, continues to define her perfect cake. Moojag gently squeezes the clip to release the key and clasps it in the palm of his hand. "I will go now," he says, slipping it into his waistcoat pocket, "to seek Kitty's approval."

"NO," screams Poof, "it's EXACTLY what she needs!"

Moojag bounces back, clutching his pocket with one hand and his hat with the other. "If you're *sûr,* Poof Poof—"

"That IS what she wants!" She springs from the chair, groping the bunch of keys and clamping it to her thigh. Moojag clasps his hands with a head wobble and hovers backwards for the entrance. "Save some for ME!" screeches Poof Poof, skipping round the intricate flower pattern laid in the wood floor. She waves and cruises to a small door at the other side of the hall.

Moojag slams the front door closed with his bum and scuttles behind a thick red curtain. "Good, the nit has gone," mumbles Poof Poof. Peeking back with a mischievous grin, she springs into the pantry. "Finally some *me* time with my favourite blueberry pancakes."

21

THE SUNSHINE VITAMIN

"My dear friends," Charlie says softly, "now you've had a good rest, it is time to replace some lost vitamin D."

The RWs reluctantly rise up and shuffle their sleepy selves behind Charlie and Biermont to door K. Charlie waves her hand over the wall's hexagonal sensory pad, and it edges open. She peeks into the Switching Room and looks back. "All clear."

"K?" asks Nema.

"K for Kitty," says Biermont. "The Switching Room is also *her* room. Aldon made her responsible for all the comings and goings."

Nema wonders where Kitty's disappeared off to now. *Good thing she was too busy watching movies to notice US coming and going. Probably poffed off for T again.*

"Back where we started," groans Izzy.

Charlie smiles, giving her a little poke. She leads them to the second door on the right, marked MT, and releases the catch. Adam reads the strange illuminated message above the door: **NOT MUSH ROOM IN 'ERE!**

He rubs his forehead and leaps in through a puff of warm air. Izzy peers into the fog as Nema jumps in front of her with a sudden burst of energy.

"It's just 'shrooms," Adam calls, poking his head back out. "*Massive* ones."

Nema nudges Izzy and leaps in. The friends wander along a humid aisle between columns of vertically growing mushrooms bathed in a soft purple light.

"The Sunshine Vitamin," announces Charlie.

Nema raises her tube to pet the silky-smooth umbrella tops with her fingertips. "Tropical," she says, crouching down to comb their dewy fanned underbelly.

"Perfect conditions," says Charlie, producing a box of perspex goggles.

Adam wipes his clammy forehead with the back of his hand. "What are those for?"

"You must wear them at once, before the pulser activates."

"Ah," pouts Adam, "the UV-zapping boost, a super-dose of Vitamin D."

Charlie nods. "Precisely. A handful of these should have

your levels back to near normal in no time." She passes them the glasses under their suits and quickly straps on her own pair. "Here it comes." She steps back as a siren sounds and an intense burst of light strikes the fungi from every angle.

"That's *it*?" asks Nema.

"Just a few seconds of the pulse," explains Charlie, "produces enough intake for a whole month."

"A handful?" asks Adam.

"More than enough."

Nema tears a family of mushrooms from the glistening patch in front of her and splits it with Izzy.

"Thanks, Nem."

"Sure."

Adam tuts, leaning in to grab some for himself from another tier.

"Out NOW, please," calls Charlie, ushering them back to the Switching Room before the vents kick back in. Izzy chokes, stuffing the remaining mushrooms into her pouch, and leaps out after her friends.

Nema pokes her head back in and inhales the pure oxygen gushing over the shrooms. She sighs, slipping out as the door slides closed. "Oxygen smells so great."

"You're so weird—I *love* it," giggles Izzy, checking her Spondylux again. "Vit D levels almost back to my normal."

"Already full over here," says Nema.

"We're going," calls Adam, following Charlie out of door T42.

Izzy chuckles at the idea of 'tea for two', while Nema's stomach growls along with PIE. *Wish she could stop thinking about food for just one minute. Makes me feel so hungry ALL of the time!*

22

POF PALACE

The Switching Room door snaps shut behind them, as they spring over the marshmallow pebbled path to Pof Palace.

"How come this lush stuff doesn't get stuck to your bottom?" Izzy calls.

"I'm not sitting on it, *am* I."

"Not your bum, Nem," explains Izzy, scouring her pouch, "your feet."

"Ah."

"It's not really marshmallow," says Adam.

"All paths should be made of marshmallow," says Nema. "Softer on your bones."

"Look," calls Izzy, squinting up at the ceiling. "There's candy in the sky *too*!"

"Welcome to Pof Palace," says Charlie, leaping through the golden gates. "Best Gajoom behaviour now." She grabs a long, chunky rope dangling by the entrance of the striped building. She pulls it down till it licks the ground and quickly lets go.

*Ding-dong ding-dong...*chimes the humungous brass bell over the door. "Again," whispers Biermont. Adam yanks up his tube to grab the rope with both hands and pulls it again.

Ding-dong...

"Pull harder," whispers Izzy.

"Give it a minute."

"We don't *have* a minute," says Nema. She leaps forward with the disguise arching over her head and clutches the rope.

Ding-dongggg ding-dongggg ding—

Izzy hops forward. "There's no one in."

"There *is*," says Nema, pointing to a small arched window above the door. She quickly pulls her disguise back down.

Izzy peeks through her mesh. "It's a little girl."

"Mummy's house," announces the rosy-cheeked child with a head full of golden ringlets.

"We need to come in, Pari," calls Charlie. "Kindly please open the door."

"I won't," replies the girl.

"But it's an emergency—" says Izzy, nudged by her friends.

The little girl scans to locate the voice. "Not allowed. Conqip says so."

"We're all in grave danger, my dear," calls Charlie. "Only our Pofs can help us. Please, Pari, let us in." The girl's sweet smile turns sour. "It's okay. No one's in trouble. We just need to find a special book." The girl turns away, disappearing from view.

She's blown it, thinks Nema. But a secret panel in the door creaks as it releases, and the edge of a battered purple wing pops out.

Charlie steps up to the door. "Poof Poof?"

"Darling, what do you want?" asks the Pof leader, chewing wildly as she pokes her head out. "I'm off to the theatre."

Charlie leans in. "We're in trouble. The Conqip are creating a Gajoom army. The Auts and the Pofs are in danger."

Poof Poof snorts. "Don't be absurd."

"It is true. We have unknowingly brought about our own destruction."

Poof Poof springs back her wings and gorges on the oozing blueberry pancakes sandwiched in her grasp. She slurps the syrup before it drips onto her tutu. "Those Auts think they know it all, but they always mess up."

"Not this time," Biermont mutters in frustration. Poof Poof screws up her nose and glares at the Gajoom.

Nema wonders about what the Auts have done. *They might have made a serious mistake, but what they learn from it will probably make them stronger. 'Everything happens for a reason.' That's what Gran always says. 'When something bad happens, something good always replaces it. You just have to notice.'*

Poof Poof squints at them and rocks her head. "Run along, to your nerdy little friends."

Charlie balks at her. "Did you *listen* to what I said? This is a crisis of the highest order. We're all very much in trouble." Nema and Izzy huddle close.

"Pofs are never in danger; the Conqip need us."

"They care about nobody but themselves."

"You're not like us," Poof Poof snaps, "nor them; you'll never be." She pops her head back inside and slams the door panel shut in Charlie's face.

"Perfect," exclaims Biermont.

Nema has another go on the rope with a massive tug lifting her off the ground. Adam watches agape as she dangles, then releases the rope, and flops down.

Ding-dongggg...

"Mummy's house. You can't come in," echoes the indifferent yelp from above.

Izzy bounds over to whisper through Nema's mesh.

"Ignore her; keep ringing."

Adam gulps, covering his eyes as Nema and Izzy lunge in for the rope.

Ding-dong ding-dongggg...

"*Mummy's* house!" calls the irritated but determined girl. "No visitors. ONLY Conqip."

"That's *it*," whispers Nema, with a triumphant wiggle.

"What's *it*?" Izzy asks, pouting.

"We pretend *we* are the Conqip." Izzy shrugs her shoulders.

"It is possible," says Charlie, nodding with a frown, "if you tell her that, she will believe it." Charlie goes for the bell again.

Ding-dong ding-dongggg...

"Mummy's house," says the deflated girl with a sigh.

Charlie looks up. "Good day, little Pari. The Conqip are here. They would like to design a splendid party just for *you*."

The girl's perky violet wings glow and shudder as she leans over the window sill. "Cake?"

"Of course—all the cake you can eat." The little girl disappears from view and the front door releases. It swings wide open, sending a gush of sweet smells pouring out.

Freshly roasted honey nuts. "*Ahhhh...*" Maple syrup pancakes. "*Mmmm...*" A wafting cheese fondue breeze. Izzy gags; Nema licks her lips; Adam nudges them both, trying not to drool.

Charlie steps through the empty doorway and signals to a stairwell at the far side of the hall. "The book is hidden in the tower."

They dash to the corner of the room and peer up the stone spiral staircase. "How many steps?" asks Izzy. "Is it dark? Are there bats? How *long* is this going to take—"

"Don't worry, Iz," says Nema shifting up her Gajoom suit and starting to climb. "I'm sure we'll be in and out in a minute."

Izzy hoists her heavy disguise and groans at Spondylux still failing to boot. "Have to eat soon, though."

"Helloooooo," a shrill voice calls from the landing, startling them all so that they nearly miss their step. "Welcome to Poof Palace."

"Wendy," utters Charlie, crushed in the Pof's bear hug.

"And you've brought your yummy Gajooms," she cries, peering over Charlie's shoulder. "I do love a Gajoom." The bright red-haired Pof, in her matching leotard and tights, grabs hold of Adam and plants a sloppy kiss on the Gajoom suit. She hovers over to Nema and gives her a squeeze. "This one's a little different?"

Charlie smiles. "Indeed."

"Cheeky little Gajooms," says the Pof, finally loosening her grip. With a wink, she turns to jab Izzy in the middle, making her jump. "I'm afraid Poof Poof has poffed off on one of her errands. Super busy running the Conqip's show." She smiles down at a fluffy, pink cloud mushrooming by her side and jabs it with her wand. It slowly disappears to reveal two small Pofs with curly, fair hair dressed in purple t-shirts and shorts: a girl, and a boy—one foot taller but with smaller wings.

"Did you give them the book, mummy?" asks Pari, the girl from the window.

Wendy kneels down and stares into her daughter's innocent eyes. "I don't *have* books, sweetheart."

"Yes, you *do*."

"No!" Wendy presses the tip of her wand into Pari's collarbone.

The flustered young Pof clutches the stick. "You *do*."

Wendy shovels her hand through her bulging pocket and showers Pari's brother with jelly babies. "Go on, Jim, tell your cheeky little sister we DON'T have books." The mellow Pof boy arcs his wing to shield himself from the candy as Izzy dreams of catching the jellies in her pouch.

"We need your help," says Charlie. "It's the Gajooms and the Auts…"

Wendy turns to grab a feather duster off the shelf behind her. "Help? What trouble are they in this time? Anyway, I couldn't even if I wanted. Poof Poof is sworn to secrecy; she never shares Conqip secrets with anyone."

Pari tugs at her mum's jittery, scarred wing. "I've seeeeeeen it."

Charlie crouches down to face the girl. "You've seen the little gold book?"

"Uh-huh. The big flying bird, too."

"She *has* seen it," says Charlie, producing a chunk of fudge brownie from her pocket. The girl peers at her brother shaking his head and quickly fixes her eyes back on mum. "Can you remember where you saw it?"

"It's impossible," snaps Wendy, darting between them. "It was destroyed."

"No," insists Charlie, "it's locked up somewhere in this palace, and I think you know where."

"Can't be. I've bleached every corner of this fabulous place. Every *inch* of it." Wendy glides her fingers over the shiny gold column beside her and presents a squeaky clean hand. "Not a speck."

"It's in the *other* tower," Pari whispers to Charlie.

"Can you show us?" The girl nods, glimpsing her mum's tight-pressed lips, and places her shaky palm on top of

Charlie's slender hand.

Nema notices the ring on the woman's fourth finger. Its small diamond twinkles as Charlie grasps the girl's little hand in hers. Nema remembers reading about marriage in PIE story. How people promised their love to each other with expensive rings. *Couldn't they have just trusted each other? I know I'd be happy with a simple hölchoko blossom. I mean, how many avocados would you have needed to even afford one of those sparkly things?*

The little girl leads them over to the stairwell with Wendy wavering behind. She points to a worn stone block in the wall. "In there, Charlie. It's in there."

23

THE BOOK

"It's inside the tunnel," whispers Pari, avoiding her mother's stare.

Charlie fingers a small hole chiselled in the stone block. "This is the special keyhole."

Nema examines the wall. *Weird place to hide a book. And Moojag, wasn't he supposed to find the key?* She turns to Charlie peering down the hall at a pink dust ball whirling like tumbleweed towards them. Wendy swings round and punches her wand into the floss to reveal the elusive Moojag. He stumbles to the floor, draws the small brass key from his waistcoat pocket and taps his nose, grinning.

"Do you know how many of these key things Poof Poof has? How does she keep track? She *cannot*." Moojag grumbles at Pari buzzing round him as he grapples with the key to line it up with the hole.

"Come, Pari," says Wendy, prodding her daughter's waist. "Let them search for their mystery book." She ushers squirming Pari down the corridor, and they shuttle out of sight.

"No time to lose," says Charlie, leaping forward. "Wendy will have no choice but to report us to Poof Poof." Moojag huffs.

"Less haste, more speed," says Nema, noticing the key slip from his fingers.

He somersaults over them, hanging upside down in the air, arms and legs crossed, coat tails flapping by his side. Charlie picks up the key and slips it straight in the hole. She turns it gently and jumps back as the block juts out and drops to the step with a thump.

"*Attention*," calls Moojag. He swoops in to catch something flying out with a tweet.

Adam gawks at the small object cradled in Moojag's hands. "Is it a book?"

"It may be small," says Charlie, "but it is great."

Nema seizes her Spondylux. "Why didn't you just find it yourselves?"

"Because we need *you* to decode its contents."

"Couldn't the Auts do that?" asks Izzy, glancing down the corridor.

"When they thought up the Gajooms," explains Charlie, "the Auts assigned a carer from the Real World to guard the Auticode, but they lost contact. She left instructions that if anything were to happen to her, they should seek out three neurodivergents."

Izzy slumps her shoulders in a sigh and leans into Adam. "Do the Auts even *want* saving? They seem happy enough to me."

"Maybe they think this is all they're good for," says Nema, "and they never thought about doing anything else, like they've lost touch with reality."

Adam rubs his chin. "It's not just the Auts in trouble, Iz, it's all of us. And anyway, it's all relative." Izzy frowns at him and gazes at Nema. "I mean," Adam adds, "how one person sees things is different to how someone else sees them."

"If they lived like us, though," says Nema, "they'd probably be a lot happier."

"Who says they're unhappy?" asks Izzy.

"Wouldn't you be, stuck down here in front of a screen, day-in-day-out, for *ten* years?" Nema looks at Moojag. *I bet no one has ever asked him what HE wants.*

"You can't force them to be like us, Nem," says Izzy, crouching to peer into the tunnel.

"Adam is right," says Charlie. "The Gajooms are multiplying of their own accord, and your world is surely in danger."

"As for the Auts," says Biermont, "a big change in their lives could be too much to bear, even a positive one."

"Nobody's forcing anyone to do anything they don't want to," says Charlie.

Nema and Izzy nudge each other. *Ha! So we get to go home now?*

"We have to trigger the Auticode first before the contest is over."

Izzy slumps with a sigh and peeks down at her skin, expecting orange only to find it stuck in her usual blue.

"The Pofs are in a talent contest tonight for the Conqip," says Biermont. "We'll activate the code then."

Charlie points at the gap in the wall. "We can't risk going back out through the Palace. The Conqip are likely on their way, so we'll take this tunnel to the lab instead."

Izzy peers inside the hole again. "Just stick your top end in," says Nema, shifting up her tube as Izzy bends over and freezes. *What if we get stuck and can't get back out? Locked inside these cold walls forever. Someone would come for us eventually, though. Wouldn't they?*

"Easier to be a round in a square," says Moojag, dithering

by the hole, "than to be square in a round."

Nema remembers Gran talking about square pegs not fitting into round holes. *She never said anything about round pegs. What even ARE pegs?*

Nema watches Izzy poke her round end into the square hole in the wall. They lift her up and cram her into the passage. Izzy squirms along, face down in the dark, and tuts at Nema's head pushing against the soles of her feet. *Did no one think of removing these tubes?* wonders Nema, as Izzy takes off in a surprisingly speedy caterpillar crawl.

With Adam, Biermont and Moojag through too, Charlie kneels down with her back to the wall. She sticks her legs in the hole and wriggles in backwards as though mailing herself through a letter box. With just her head and arms left poking out, she reaches down to lift the surprisingly light stone. She fumbles to wedge in the block after her and a shaft of light beams through the gap where it's left jutting out.

WHAM!

Izzy growls, head bent against a dead end. "GO BACK," she calls with everyone piled up behind her.

"I think she's hit a wall," says Adam, squished between Nema and Biermont.

Izzy wriggles inside her disguise to pull her hood up over her head. Its cells inflate, spawning knobby ridges like sea coral. She cocks her head and butts the wall, dislodging the block and nudging it out. Nema watches her puffed-up friend slink out after it into a small, lamp-lit room with nothing but the four cold stone walls and another spiral staircase in the corner.

If we were in a cartoon—which wouldn't surprise me— Izzy'd have a halo of birdies tweeting over her right now.

Gran was right, love: PIE *is* 'tougher than any armour ever invented'.

Nema drops out of the hole and drags herself away from the wall. "Down dog, Iz," she says, pushing off the ground into an upside down V shape.

Izzy chuckles, joining her. "Down Gajoom—"

"*Pas oublier de respirer*," chants Moojag, diving in to mirror their pose. "Remember to breathe in, and breathe out too…"

Adam smirks at the colourful row of sticky, stripy, and velvety bums sticking up in the air. "I guess we should take a look at this book," he says, eyeballing Biermont.

"Coming through," calls Charlie, the soles of her purple pumps peeking out the tunnel.

Nema jumps up and leaps over to grab the woman's feet.

"She's coming out breech. She could get stuck and stop breathing."

It seems my dear girl has gone into birthing auto-pilot.

"I think the lack of oxygen has gone to your head, Nem," says Adam. He helps her gently rotate Charlie out of the hole.

"Hmm, a wall giving birth," says Izzy, watching slender Charlie flop out the tunnel like a sugar-coated, slippery eel. "That's a first."

Charlie squints up at Nema and Adam. "Thanks, my friends, for…well, thanks."

"Sure," says Nema, brow raised. "We've delivered lots of babies. Cows, deer, cats, and dogs too…but this has to be our very first *wall* birth."

Charlie smiles, leaning forward to poke the hat dangling between Moojag's arms. Still in down-dog position, he flips back up and retrieves the book from his jacket pocket. "Over and out," he says, jabbing Adam's middle with it.

Charlie gets up, placing her hands in her pockets. "You can skip your disguises in here. The Conqip would never fit in that tunnel."

Adam whips off the sticky tube and accepts the golden book from Moojag with a mutual nod. He rests it on the palm of his hand and reaches for his Spondylux. Nema shakes her head, waving her idle shell at him.

"*Vite, vite,*" urges Moojag, "unclose the book."

Nema tries to imagine books always open, never closed. At least, that's what she thinks he means. *Must be tricky being yourself down here with the controlling Conqip. If Gran was still around, she'd have thought him 'brave' too.*

Well, your mum certainly does.

Adam tucks his thumb under the stiff cover to flip it over. "Watch out!" cries Nema, as a star shoots out.

Colourful sparks rocket from the book's quivering pages, as the cover flips open-closed-open-closed-open, and a fiery wheel spirals out and up over their heads.

"Stunning little thing, isn't it," whispers Charlie, seeing Nema jump back and Moojag bob up and down.

Did books always explode in your face like this? No wonder people had such a hard time giving them up.

Charlie taps her forehead. "Books have a mind of their own now, of course."

Adam gawks back at her. "Of course."

"*Mais oui,*" chants Moojag, "anything is possible."

Nema peers over Adam's shoulder as he dares to turn the page. He pinches the corner and turns it over. The others lurch forward to gaze at the sketch before them: a sweeping mountain and a wooden house with a sloping roof at its peak. "Chalet?" Nema asks.

"You probably should," mumbles Izzy, savouring her last toffee. "Not very colourful, is it."

"Chalet," repeats Nema, recalling the day Gran left them for Swiss Tops. "And there's nothing wrong with black and white."

Charlie points to the drawing and nods to Adam. "Touch it."

Nema wonders if it's like those children's books she's seen on PIE story, the ones with magnetic ink. *The page looks so smooth and soft; I bet he's dying to touch it.*

Adam frowns, lowering his finger to the page. He lightly presses the paper and bolts back as a big blue-green spark bursts from the mountain. Nema leans in quickly to tap the building. When she lifts her finger, the wooden house fills, plank by plank, with the silvery hues of weathered eucalyptus. Izzy pokes the landscape, flooding it with frosty greens, while a crisp winter sunset gradiates the sky.

Nema glances at Izzy's scrunched up face and back at a tiny black spot emerging over the picture's horizon. It grows into a tiny bird, unfurling its wings and ruffling the pages before flying out and transforming into a majestic two-headed eagle.

"Turn the page, Adam," says Izzy, ducking out of its way as it sweeps over them.

"I can't," he answers, tugging at the stubborn corner.

"Come, *monsieur*." Adam buries his chin in his chest and sighs. "You must will it," says Moojag, "and it will come."

"Will it?" asks Adam, glancing at Izzy.

"*I* don't know, *will* it?"

"He means, 'will' it," says Nema, remembering Morag's coaching, "as in *really* wanting it." She closes her eyes and focuses on the rhythm of her breath. Her mind clears faster this time than the last, and the book begins to rumble in Adam's hand.

"*C'est ca*, you've got it," beams Moojag, spinning round Adam while the page, as if by magic, flips right over. "You see what is the happenings when your brain puts to it?"

Adam glares at the animated book turning its own pages. "But I didn't—"

"Just a bunch of stupid numbers," Izzy says, studying the page full of bold black digits.

Adam bites his lip, scanning the grid with his jelly-like finger. "There's a pattern."

Nema immediately recognises the string of numbers. "It's the Fibonacci."

"Fiba-*what*?" asks Izzy, squinting at her friends.

"You *know*, FI-BO-NA-CHI?"

Moojag swoops in, circling an imaginary wand in the air. "Spirals and patterns, my friends; the sequence of nature whereby each number is the sum of the preceding two."

Nema points a lit-up grey finger in the air to draw the numbers, as Moojag explains the rule.

"*Alors*...0+1=1, 1+1=2, 1+2=3, 2+3=5, 3+5=8...13, 21, 34...and so on and so forth." Charlie and Biermont gawk at the string of glowing digits now bobbing in front of them. Moojag claps his hands and bows to Nema. "We have holograms too, yes we do, but not emit from our fingers like you. Cuckoo."

Izzy paces, flicking her shell. "What've fibona-chi's got to do with anything?"

Nema grasps Adam's hand and, without even closing her eyes, wills the page right over. Adam and Izzy stare at the photo before them of a younger Moojag. He's no more than eight years old with a tanned complexion, scooped button nose, and silky, long black hair—centre-parted like hooked-back curtains, barely tucked behind his ears.

They turn, incredulous, to study Nema's face. She rubs her tingling skin and checks her Spondylux, but it's as good as dead. Her legs feel shaky, her head heavy. She squints back at the blurring photograph and leans into Adam. *Moojag looked just like me when he was small. Who is he?*

Yes, my love, you are so much alike.

Nema raises the water bottle grasped in her sweaty grip to her pursed, dry lips and sips the last drop. Suddenly, she turns her gaze towards me. She can *see* me standing here. She looks across at Moojag. "Is he the boy? Your boy?" she whispers, glancing back at me as I glide over to him. "*Our* boy. Is he…?"

Yes, my love. Yes.

"It's *you*," whispers Izzy, peering at my girl's face as Moojag hovers forward, palms pressed together. "I saw it at Box Hill. You two are like twins—"

"*Non*," says Moojag, glancing at Nema, "not her. It is *me*."

Nema climbs up and leans against the wall. *Mum? Is it really you?* I blow her a kiss, Moojag too, but the vision of me must already have vanished.

"Next page, dear Moojag," says Charlie, pulling them away to give my girl space. Moojag swiftly turns the page, darts behind Adam, and peers unsettled over his shoulder.

"It's us!—" Izzy calls, poking Nema. But my girl just flinches and turns away.

"The SAs guessed that one day they would lose their intuition," explains Charlie, "their ability to sense others' thoughts and feelings. So when they made the Gajooms, they also created the Auticode in case anything should go wrong. They entrusted the Carer to protect it."

Izzy sticks her hands on her hips. "So, who *is* this Carer?"

"We aren't sure. She disappeared four years ago. But she chose three Real Worlders to reverse the code when the time came, and she hid the clues in this book."

"*Us,* you mean," says Adam. "So we sort of inherited the book?"

"*Tourne la page*—turn the page," says Moojag, pacing. Adam, with a little invisible help from my girl, quickly turns to the next page and a picture of the Real World with the letters **N-A-I** projecting out like a Hola.

"We were to seek a twelve-year-old girl whose name begins with N," explains Biermont, "and her two friends, A and I."

"She said we would find you together," adds Charlie, "and that you would know."

Izzy shrugs her shoulders at the blank Spondylux, while Adam passes Nema his water and puts his arm around her.

My girl gazes across at Moojag. *Is HE the boy she wanted me to find? Is SHE his mum, too? Is he MONZI?*

I left her world when she was just three. The only memory she has of me is from the night before the Great Surge at Hampstead Top, wrapped up in my warm embrace. That special hug has stayed with her always. My face, though, was forgotten long ago. There have been no pictures or words to remind her. She always thought the memories were too painful for her father, but now she senses there's another reason—the reason no one ever talks about me or my dear boy, Monzi.

Moojag twirls to a halt and prods Nema's shoulder. "Should you not help us, the consequence your world will experience too soon." He flops to the floor but scrambles straight back up at a thunderous blow shaking the ground.

Charlie lowers her ear to the tunnel and jerks at the sound of a rumbling block. "Disguises back on!"

"Time to go," whispers Izzy, gripping Nema's arm.

"Is he—"

"Yes, it's me, Iz-zy. Now come on!"

24

THE AUTICODE

Adam and Izzy hop down the stairs. Nema watches their shadows cloak the curved wall as they disappear out of sight. "The chalet," she says, following behind Biermont and Moojag.

"Yes?" asks Charlie.

"Gran moved to Swiss Tops two years ago. She never posted any photos, but she described it just like the place in the picture."

"Where is she now?"

Nema pauses on the bottom step. The familiar SA sign glows on the wall in front of her. *Where IS Gran? Wish she were here right now. She'd know what to do, what to say. I miss her.*

You're so close, my love. Don't give up now.

"She sent a Hola after she left. We never heard from her again. The message was strange. Something about a secret and a bank account." *Dad never did work out what it meant. He just said it was 'for the best'. Best what, though?*

Adam peers down the long corridor they first took to the lab as Nema reaches the bottom of the stairwell. She calls "Gran's letter" and pulls up her disguise. "It's in French," she says, pointing to the Hola.

Moojag rocks forward to explore the lit message hovering beside them, but his excited grin quickly turns to a frown. Everyone leans in to inspect the words and glare at one in big bold letters: **CONQIP**. *The Hola was where my girl heard the name before.*

Moojag flaps his hands. "This letter is TOP secret! It tells the account number from a Swiss bank where they hoarded stolen *milliards* before the catastrophe."

"Stolen billiards?" asks Izzy, fumbling with her shell and crossing her arms in a huff.

Nema sighs. "*Milliards*, Iz. 'Billions' in English. Not 'billiards'."

Moojag spins off. "What else does it say?" asks Charlie, drawing him back in.

Moojag probes his jacket's multiple inner pockets and

pulls out a little magnifying glass. "An experiment," he calls, zooming in, "on autistic children."

"The Auts?" asks Izzy.

"*Non*. Little girls with difficulties to walk. The Zizanth cured them, but then they were never seen again."

"And where does Nema's gran fit in with all this?" Adam asks Charlie.

"It appears she was the mystery Carer."

Adam shuffles closer to Nema. "So she *knew* about this place?"

"It seems she knew too much," says Biermont, frowning at Moojag. "Why she had to leave."

My girl bows her head. *How could Gran be involved in an experiment on children?*

"But there's more," says Izzy, lifting up her tube to clasp Nema's hands in hers.

"*Moment…*"

"You don't have to read it…if you don't want to," says Nema, gasping as my voice whirs on in her head: 'Forgive me…I was weak…you are strong.' My girl wishes she could just switch me off. She's lost the energy to work. Staring at the outline of the panel in the wall, she imagines smashing through and sprinting out of here, not stopping until she's safely back in RW.

"*Un petit garçon*—a small boy," says Moojag, struggling to read on as he realises what it means.

Nema lowers her eyes. "My brother, Monzi. He went into a clinic when he was six. They said he had an infectious disease and wasn't allowed home. Then he just vanished with the Surge. Mum went searching for him, and then we lost her too. Dad never talks about them." She glances earnestly at Moojag. "He would've turned eighteen yesterday. I'd forgotten the date. Gran said never to forget his birthday."

Moojag sinks to his knees as the Hola fizzles out. Izzy crouches beside him, looking round at Nema. "What is it?"

"It's the letter, Iz. It's upset him." Nema isn't ready to share the news that she has just found her long lost brother, that he's right there beside her, alive and well, and he is— MOOJAG.

Charlie offers my shocked boy her hand and pulls him in close. As he rests his head against her silky thigh, she looks to Adam and Izzy. "Don't forget, you're all part in this puzzle. What in the book spoke to you two?"

"Said nothing to me," Izzy croaks, nudging Nema as she sucks on her last mint.

"Must be something," says Charlie. "Anything in the book that you recall from your childhood?"

Izzy shuts her eyes for a moment. "Could be the bird.

There was this one photograph my grandma took in Kenya. It was a big kite eagle, double-headed just like the one from the book. I always hated those four beady eyes staring right at me."

Adam scratches his forehead. "I remember that. I'm pretty sure it was *my* grandmother's. Anyway," he says, shaking his head, "maybe it has something to do with those numbers." Nema gawks at her friends. She remembers *her* gran talking about Kenya, too.

Focus on the code, my love. Answers will come—all in good time.

Izzy raises her arm inside the disguise to feel for Spondylux. She huffs at it still refusing to power up. "We can do this without Spondy," says Nema, biting her lower lip as a burst of energy rushes through her. "What do Fibonacci and Switzerland have in common?"

"Fibonacci numbers have something in common with just about everything," says Adam.

"Fair. How about Kenya and Switzerland, then?"

"Well, yes, as it goes—the famous 'Kenyan billions'," says Adam, doing a jiggle. "The richest lot stashed all their money in a single Swiss bank account before the Surge.

It was all over *whatsnapchatvibeinstatwitface*. A statement got leaked right before the Great Power Cut. And get this—the bank's logo was an eagle."

Nema points to the double-headed eagle in Gran's Hola with the words **TARTE BANQUE** wrapped round it. Izzy mumbles, savouring the last morsel of candy on her tongue. "Tart, huh?"

Moojag chews on a strand of hair as he examines Gran's profile in the message. "The code," he mutters. "You will find it there—in the account number."

Nema wonders how he even knows that. *Did Gran tell him? What's he even doing down here? And if Gran knew he was here, how come she never told us?*

"How about," suggests Adam, "we match up this account's numbers with the Fibonacci ones."

Nema reads out the numbers. "1-0-6-0-4-2-1-3."

"Are we doing a new fibo-whatsie?" asks Izzy.

"You can't do a new Fibonacci," says Adam. "The Fibonacci *is* the Fibonacci. You can't just change its numbers."

"Sometimes," says Biermont, "we get so stuck on what we know, we miss the very possibilities staring us in the face."

"Sometimes people are so quiet," says my girl, "when

they *do* speak, it's like there's a 'ghost stalker' in the room."

"Nema!"

"It's okay, Adam," whispers Biermont, "I got her."

"You do?"

"Sure," he says, nudging Nema. "Sometimes you gotta just go with your gut."

Izzy rubs her belly. "Mine says hungry."

Nema glances at her. "Your gut can wait. What if we match up the numbers?"

Adam nods as Moojag flips upside down and hovers over him in tree pose. "Let's see now, that would be: zero and one but not six, 'cause six isn't in the Fibonacci. Neither is four. Which leaves just two…and three?"

"0-1-2-3? But that's too easy?" says Izzy.

"It's cunningly simple," says Biermont. Moojag spins and grins. The problem-solving has given my lovely boy a boost.

"I suppose it is," says Charlie, steadying Moojag as he flops back down. "And the Kenyans' account?"

They all turn to Nema. "Don't look at me, I'm back to zero charge."

"Whose bright idea was this?" huffs Izzy.

"Actually," says Adam, "I've got it stored."

Izzy pictures their friend's smug face. "Not much use if you're out of charge too."

"Not in PIE's memory—in my head! I see the numbers as clear as a kalokairi day." Adam focuses on the image in his mind's eye: **029-0126793**

"Zero—yes, two—yes, nine—no…" he says, checking Charlie's stunned face. "Zero—yes, one—yes, two—yes, six—no, seven—no, nine—no, three—yes."

"0-1-2-3 again," says Nema.

Charlie circles her arm to release the round panel in the wall and clasps her hands as it rotates up. "Well done, friends. Now to stripe up every last Gajoom and reverse that code before it's too late. Conqip will soon be on their way; we must hurry."

Moojag swerves round her and climbs through, glancing back at Nema with a frown before disappearing into the glare of the lab.

25

SUPER SENSE

"Time to apply the special code," announces Charlie, stepping last into the lab. "With your help, we'll get this reversal completed in no time. But first we must gather all the Gajooms."

"Isn't that the Auts' job?" asks Nema.

"Well, for this, we need *all* hands on deck."

Nema sighs, looking down at her trapped hands. *That Charlie really loves a challenge.*

"Of course, you'll have to remove your disguises, but not till all Gajooms are present. And, we must take care. It will upset the Auts to learn they've caused stress to the Gajooms."

"They're very sensitive, then?" asks Adam.

Nema nudges him. *Why is he even saying that? The Auts probably wouldn't BE Auts if they weren't so sensitive.*

Charlie nods. "They are. In fact, they have hypersensitivity, which at times is so overwhelming that their feelings spiral quite out of control."

Nema wonders if the Auts just go along with this because they're so tuned-in to stuff, like when she's working. "Doing the same thing over and over," she says, "must help them switch off."

"That's how they sit here every day just coding, then?" asks Izzy, fidgeting with her shell.

"Pretty much," answers Charlie. "It's logical work, predictable too. That helps them feel more in control. But they're really good at it, because they see things differently. Ideas that seem obvious to them just don't make sense to others. But that can make someone feel like they're doing something wrong, when in fact the opposite is true."

Nema looks down, shaking her head. *Must be hard...when other people don't get you...like what you're saying doesn't make any sense. Imagine not understanding yourself or just how amazing you are...*

"Many of the Auts don't need mathematical formulas to solve problems," says Biermont. "It comes so naturally, they often can't even explain how they do it. We believe it has something to do with their twenty-second sense."

"Huh? They have more than seven?" asks Izzy, wide-eyed.

"Everyone does," says Adam.

"As well as 'proprioceptive' and 'vestibular'—" says Nema, "the ones that help you move and balance—you've also got 'crono-' something and 'magneto-' thingamajiggy... There are at least twenty-one."

Charlie nods, smiling. "Someone *has* done their homework."

Nema squints at the woman. She's never heard of homework. *Does Charlie mean dreaming? In PIE? Because PIE is home, and I'm pretty much always working. So yes, Charlie—I'm doing my home work all the time!*

"Well," Biermont continues, "they discovered the Auts had an additional super sense." Izzy turns to watch the busy Auts, tapping away at their keyboards. "We found that the Auts could read others' emotions, even predict future events. The difficulty was, they either weren't aware of their gift or they couldn't control it. That scared them so much they were forced to bury it—pretend it didn't exist."

Nema wonders if having seen the lighthouse, and me, and being able to turn pages means she has this special sense too. *What happened to the Auts' super sense? Do they still have it? Could they get it back if someone helped them—the way Morag helped me?*

Yes, love, you can always get it back if you want it enough.

"So why on earth," asks Adam, rubbing his forehead, "are the Auts down here, doing *this?*"

"When the people running the world discovered the super sense, they panicked," says Biermont. "They feared the trouble it might cause them. But because the children were so afraid of the things they could do, it was easy for the Conqip to offer them a distraction, an escape from a world that didn't understand them."

Charlie looks around at the Auts. "We have to remind them of their strengths, show them how they can be their true selves in the Real World." She winks at the smallest worker at a station in the corner fidgeting on his ball. The familiar figure peeks at them from beneath his top hat.

Nema leaps over to my boy. "You're a worker? An SA?"

Silence…

"It's me, Nema," she whispers, "your—" Moojag huddles over his perspex desk, shooing her away.

"Burnout," explains Charlie, stepping over. "He's overwhelmed from the past few days. He's also not used to you seeing him as an Aut."

My girl looks into his tired eyes. *He took a big risk coming up to the Real World to find us. He's exhausted after everything he's seen, having met new people and then finding me. Sometimes I have to switch off too, when there's a lot going on in my head.*

"He won't mind me saying," adds Charlie, "that being away from his station for a while can affect his mood."

"But he seems *much* quieter," says Izzy, hopping over and scouring her empty pouch. "Not his usual, fun self."

"He's an Aut," says Nema. "He needs time to recharge. Like us, except he doesn't have PIE to warn him when he's low on energy." *Gran must have given him to the Conqip. Did Mum know?*

Charlie holds her hand out to my boy. "You're probably still trying to process the letter, dear Mooj', aren't you? It's okay," she says, turning to the friends. "He'll share whatever it is with us in his own time."

Moojag drops down off his ball and peers up at Charlie. He slips a hand in his waistcoat pocket and probes her palm with the other, forcing a smile back at Nema.

"Shall we reverse this code?" Charlie asks. Moojag bows his head and hops back to his PC. He frantically enters the digits and rocks on his ball, nibbling on a nail as he waits.

"*Complet*," he announces, folding up his arms. Across the room, a giant throbbing 3D print station jets out continuous streams of sweet-smelling, violet strips. Izzy bounds straight over to the machine with Moojag moping after her. "The anti-code," he says as she squats by the pile. "*Délicieux* liquorice stripes."

"Don't eat them, Iz!" calls Nema, recalling the *glyko riza*.

Moojag bows his head. "Eat as much as you wish—if you are Gajoom."

"I'm *not* Gajoom, Moojag; you know that."

"Well, you look like one."

Izzy pouts, turning to Charlie. "So what *do* we do with these strips?"

"You must grab a Gajoom and roll it up in one."

Nema gasps. *Surely there's a gentler way?*

Charlie catches a strip before it drops to the floor. "Don't worry, they receive all their codes this way. Before they know it, the replicating action will be reversed. They will simply default to their peaceful candy-generating selves."

Charlie turns to the Auts. "Sparky, Sparkles—where are you? We need your assistance most urgently!" Izzy peers across the room to two quivering Auts crouching on the floor below the rectangular clock.

"Over there," says Moojag, "wasting time."

"Thanks a lot," grumbles Sparkles.

Nema frowns. *I'm not sure they want to be found. And how can they possibly be 'wasting' time?*

"Sparkles, Sparky—we must wrap up the Gajooms. I know it's not their usual feed time, but this is an emergency, and you are their favourites, so—"

Sparkles whimpers, glancing at her brother, his head clasped in his hands. "But he's not in the right mood."

"It'll be over before you can say 'Jiminy Cricket'," calls Biermont.

"JIMINY CRICKET!" cry the siblings.

"Oh, no—not literally, my dears," says Charlie.

"Not that stupid literal business again," moans Sparkles. "You people really gotta say what you mean. Okay?"

Sparky frowns and circles a raised finger. "Pinocchio's official conscience, of course," explains Sparkles. "Never ever harm a cricket, Sparky. They're full of positive energy and good luck."

Charlie strides over to the pair. "You won't have to speak to anyone."

Sparkles gazes up at her and pouts. "No words?"

"Not even one. I just need you to round up the Gajooms and bring them in right away. But the Conqip mustn't know," she says, tapping her nose.

Sparky turns to his sister, copying Charlie. "She's got an itch or something."

"It's our secret," explains Charlie. "You mustn't tell a soul that we are reversing the code. You can just tell the Gajooms it is their feed time, okay?"

Sparky raises a brow at his sister. "So we *do* have to talk!" yells Sparkles, turning to Charlie, arms crossed. "And it's not feed time—that's lying!"

Charlie steers their gaze to the swelling mountain of jumbo candy strips. "Oh my," exclaims Sparkles, "that is an immense amount of liquorice!" Sparky puffs his cheeks, throwing his arms out in front of him.

"It wouldn't be wise to tell them they'll get fat," says Charlie.

"You're saying he's STUPID!?" says Sparkles glaring at her.

"Of course not," says Charlie, pressing her hand to her chest. "I want you for this delicate task precisely because you are *not*."

Sparkles glances round at her brother. "She's not having a heart attack, is she?"

Charlie takes a moment to carefully select her words. "I just believe in you two bravelings." She bites her lip at her poor choice.

Sparky glares at his sister, shaking his head. "*Meh,*" huffs Sparkles, "*not* a word, but all right, brave woman."

"Good, so it's settled then?" smiles Charlie.

Sparky huffs, crossing his arms. "Come on," says Sparkles, patting his shoulder, "let's get it over with."

Sparky lifts a hand to his face and, with finger and thumb shaped in the letter C, taps his chin. "Fine, my brother," says Sparkles, nodding with Charlie, "we'll get you chocolate."

They clamber up and follow her to another perspex chute suspended from the ceiling in the corner of the lab. Sparkles lays on the ground beside her brother under the big transparent tube. "How many?"

"All of them," answers Biermont. "Be sure to collect every single last one."

The pair stick their legs inside and hover upside down, hair flying round their faces. "Only the last one, then," calls Sparkles. "You can only have *one* last one. What if everyone was last? Seriously, where would they all go? You could stack 'em up high, I suppose—"

"*All* of them, Sparkles."

"Say what you mean, then. Anyway, I'm not taking instructions from a Gajoom." Sparkles wiggles an arm out to prod G21. "Hang on!" she says, turning to Sparky, "Since when did we get the Gajooms to speak?"

Charlie pokes her head inside the chute next to Sparkles' upside down face. "He's not a Gajoom."

"What *is* he then?"

"One of us," answers Charlie, her short silver hair sticking up punk.

Sparkles and Sparky snigger, their faces blushing from the blood rushing south. "My brother says 'Stop pretending you're something you're not'."

"Remember," says Charlie, crawling back out, "if anyone comes in, you're just rounding up Gajooms for their feed."

Sparky mutters something angrily as he grips on tightly to his sister, and they shoot up for the ceiling. "That's all right," cries Sparkles. "I'll do the talking. Could use the practice any*waaaayyyy...*"

26

SPARKS FLY

Sparkles and Sparky fly round the bend of the tunnel and hover down the other side, before landing softly on their feet. Sparky crawls out after Sparkles and stumbles into the factory. They check the doors and head for the throng of Gajooms jostling beside the conveyor belt.

"I'll go up front," says Sparkles. "You go to the back of the line."

Sparky shakes his head and sighs.

"They will. They always move, just like we programmed them—to follow like sheep."

Sparky shakes his head, pointing to his mouth.

"Hopefully they won't notice it's *not* the proper feed time," says Sparkles. Sparky sighs. *He's right, though*, thinks Sparkles, *especially if they're moodier now, and more anxious…They love their routine too.* "We'll be super gentle and take it real slow, just like when we trained them."

"Taki…wā…tanga?"

"Exactly right, Sparky. Yes, they'll come in their own good time."

(*Takiwātanga* is the Māori word for autism, it means 'in your own time and space'. That thoughtful Keri Opai and the disabled community made it up for the Te Reo Hāpai dictionary.)

The siblings creep up to the sticks. "Hey, Gajooms, it's time for your special liquorice feed."

The sticks jolt upright. "They're not sure, Sparks."

Sparky raises a finger.

"You want to try luring one over, first? Nice—then the rest should follow." Sparky grins nodding.

"I've got some delicious liquorice for you," Sparkles informs the Gajoom heading the line.

Sparky watches his sister gesture to the stick and edge back. The Gajoom twists round and follows her to the chute. He sneaks to the end of the line, grabbing a massive chocolate coin from the conveyor on his way. He repeats the trick with the last Gajoom at the belt. This one also turns and follows him before heading off after the other Gajooms to the chute. The next in line instinctively bolts off, then the next and the next, each following the one before it.

As the siblings drive round the last wandering sticks, Sparkles spies some stray from the neat line up. She glances over her shoulder at the door. The pink light flashes and the tannoy speaker rattles out the anthoom. She grabs Sparky's arm and pulls him in close.

The factory door swings open and Aldon strides in, raising his champagne flute. "Once these Gajooms get replicating and nasty, we can just sit back as they set to work wrecking the grotty RW."

"Perfection, A—though wouldn't an army of Brixes have been a touch more glamorous..."

Travis mopes in, sweeping back his hair. "Seems a shame; grown rather fond of the stripy folk."

"You've turned *rather* soppy in your old age," says Brix.

"Excuse *me*," huffs Travis, reworking his limp quiff as he checks himself in the mirrored door. "Sorry for caring."

"Who said anything about *caring?*" retorts Aldon. "Sympathise? *Hmm*, perhaps. But empathise? With *that* lot? Not on your nelly!"

Brix turns back to face the door and admires his pale pink shirt in the reflection. "Lest we forget: they're only stupid sticks of rock."

"Get it over with, though, will you?" says Travis, tipping his empty glass, "I don't fancy being left down here, thirsty and starving."

"Don't be so pathetic," says Aldon. "Soon we'll have total control over everything and everyone, underground and overground. Everyone else doing all the work—as it *ought* to be." He raises his flute and sniggers, clinking glasses with Brix. They gulp down the remaining fizz in one and turn onto the factory floor.

"Something's up," says Brix, pouting at the idle Gajooms dotted around the chute.

Travis follows behind, pinching a cherry tart off the moving belt. "Perhaps they're taking some sort of break?"

"AUTISTS!" shouts Aldon, furiously shaking his fists at the hunched pair. Sparkles and Sparky turn to face him, nodding back feebly.

Brix smirks at them. "SORRY, what was that? Did you *say* something?" Travis sniggers at Sparkles rattling her head.

Aldon clenches his teeth and turns to Brix. "I simply will NOT tolerate discourtesy. Find out what's going on here before I do something you will *all* regret."

"Darling, darling Auts," says Brix, pulling a crooked smile, "ought you not greet your leader with a touch more politeness? You're both very sensitive, we know. So endearing," he adds with alarming charm. "I'm sure we can't imagine what it's like to be so *slow*. But you can *always* share your troubles with us."

Sparky shuffles behind his sister, clinging to her sleeve as Travis leans in with a smirk. "The old sweet-talk not having its usual effect today, Brix?"

Aldon's head looks as though it might pop. "For god's sake, Auts, RESPOND, will you? Like NORMAL people."

"Liquorice," whispers Sparkles, "feed."

"*Feed*? I suppose that's your mono-syllabic way of telling me it's their feeding time?" Aldon doesn't bother to wait for a response. "Does this not take place at thirty-four hours?"

"System was down," Sparkles answers stiffly.

Sparky frowns, shaking his head.

"*Shhh*," Sparkles hisses at her brother.

"WELL?" demands Aldon, diving in for Sparky's cringing face and cocking an ear to Sparkles' quivering lips. "*Was* it down or NOT?"

"Yeah," she answers, squeezing Sparky's frail arm so hard he can barely feel it. "Tech issue. Feeding 'em now; all good."

Aldon rolls his eyes and shoos them away with his cane. "Get on with your ridiculous task, then. And it's 'yes', not 'yeah'."

Travis floats like a pesky mosquito behind the expressionless pair as they tip-toe wearily back to the

Gajooms. "THANK YOU?" They pause in their tracks, hearts pounding, and gaze at each other puzzled.

"For goodness' sake, Auts," Brix sniffs, "just respond appropriately, would you? Like REGULAR folk."

Travis shakes his head, turning for the belt. "Ungrateful."

"Sad, really," adds Aldon, tilting his head to catch a response. "After ALL we've done for them."

"Thank you," mumbles Sparkles, nudging her brother's trembling shoulder.

"Thanks," utters Sparky.

Aldon grunts, returning to his sniggering oafs. "Let's go pay the lab a visit, shall we? Check on progress. But first, young men—a spot of Gajoomdom Gin?"

"Marvellous," says Travis. "Bets on which dumb Aut we can get to speak first?"

"Fabulous," snickers Brix, "my favourite sport. I'm willing to give you my little blonde Pof Dina, if you win."

"With the buck teeth?" asks Travis, curling his thin top lip to expose his rotten, cavity-filled mouth.

Brix winces at the stench of his breath. "She's not perfect, sure, but she's fresh and *soooo* easy to shape."

The Conqip, you see, have this wicked habit of picking out Pofs as their pets. The Pofs are so chill and fun to be around, and they'll do anything a Conqip asks. But the Conqip get

211

bored after a while. Then they ghost them as though they never existed.

"Okay, you're on," agrees Travis. "And if you win, which is bloody unlikely, you can have Debs."

"You mean Ginge?" Travis nods. "Fair enough," says Brix, turning around. "You in too, boss?"

Aldon grabs their shoulders and thrusts them out the room. "You kids enjoy yourselves, why don't you, while I do all the hard work."

Travis jerks, half-expecting Aldon's usual slap. "Suit yourself."

***

Sparkles wipes her brow. "We have to get back to the lab before the Conqip, or we're done for."

Sparky sniffs, swiping his finger across his throat.

"They won't kill you," says Sparkles, looking up at the crimson ceiling. "I do wonder sometimes if it might be easier."

Sparky stops to feel his sister's words and squints with a forced smile. He points to himself, crosses his arms over his chest, and points back at hers.

Sparkles smiles. "I love you, too." She crosses her arms over her chest and points back at him. "Come on then—

let's sort out these Gajooms."

Sparky signals to the group pushed right up into the corner.

"Must have got scared with all the yelling and scattered," says Sparkles. She tries steering them out, but they won't budge. Sparky grabs a flashlight from the shelf and shines it over the chute. "Brilliant, Sparks—there are way more lights on at the usual feed time."

One Gajoom, seeing the chute light up, leaps over and ducks to enter but hesitates. Sparky taps his temple before crouching to inspect the chute. Something still isn't right. He peers at the launch pad and pinches his nose as he pokes its squeaky clean surface.

"Is it too fresh?" asks Sparkles.

Sparky nods, clamping his mouth now too, from the reeking new-rubber smell. He yanks away the pad and replaces it with an old tacky one, left festering to the side. The Gajoom cheerfully leaps onto the familiar worn-edged material, and Sparkles stoops into the tunnel beside it.

"See you over there, Sparky." Sparkles clings to the Gajoom and zooms up the chute with it. One by one, the others follow. The last few sticks dotted about the room finally bound up to the sticky pad and launch themselves for the lab.

"One left!" Sparky hollers up the tube.

Charlie's voice bounces back round the bend. "Good work, just sneak up from behind and give it a nice big push." Sparky clamps his head in his hands.

"Don't worry, Sparks," echoes his sister's voice. "It won't notice 'cause of its numb spot."

Sparky hesitates a moment, trying to remember where the numb spot is. He knows it's its back side of course, but he's always had trouble figuring out this sort of stuff—like his left from his right and a Gajoom's back from their front.

As you've probably worked out, they look pretty much the same all the way round. But sometimes something is so simple it gets confusing when you think about it for too long, doesn't it?

Sparky ponders, as the unnerved Gajoom retreats from the chute. "Thank you!" he calls out, remembering how they always travel in the same direction. He tip-toes round the stick and, with all his might, lunges at its middle, sending it bolting onto the launch pad with barely a *joom* and plenty of *stik*.

He jumps in, flinging his spindly arms around it, not even caring he'll get sticky. He clings on tight and squeals as they hurtle up through the ceiling and fly round the bend. A blast of air shoots up the tunnel, suspending them midway and gently setting them back down on the lab floor. The upside down Gajoom (yes, they do indeed look the same both ways up) slips out the chute, with Sparky still clinging on, and flips them both back upright.

Moojag is hurriedly herding the jumbled Gajooms away from the chute, and the RWs are helping Biermont rally round the Auts. Charlie helps pull Sparky off from the stick. "Nice work. Did you count?" She turns to Sparkles for the answer.

Sparkles glares back wide-eyed at her brother and gasps bending over. "Didn't think…Got caught...Conqip on their way."

27

AUT TO CONVINCE

Charlie turns from the returned siblings to the other Auts. "Now is a special time for us *all*." The Auts look to each other, the clock, and suspiciously back at the heaving bunch of sticks. "You see there's another, better society. It's called RW—Real World. Overground." She pauses to give them time.

Sparkles looks at her brother shaking his head. "But we're fine with things just how they are."

"You're far more than coders, you know." The room fills with frowns and shrugged shoulders. "Every one of you has untapped potential and—"

"We're *lazy,*" declares an Aut at the back.

"Good for nothing," agrees her neighbour.

"We've got everything we need down here," says another, echoing the Conqip. "Too much interaction is no good for us."

"You were chosen for your incredible problem-solving

skills," says Charlie, "but you're so much more."

Sparkles skips forward, breaking the awkward silence. "We're *sensitive*, Charlie, aren't we?"

"Absolutely—"

"Amazing sensory powers?" she says with a glint in her eye.

Charlie frowns at Sparkles' grumbling brother. "You too, Sparky. Your intuitiveness is what makes *you* so special. Feeling intensely makes you strong, not weak."

Sparky looks at his sister, pointing to Charlie and circling a finger at his tilted head. Sparkles gawks back at him with twitchy eyes. "She's not crazy, Sparks."

"Charlie *is* right," calls an Aut, poking her head out the crowd. "We get what others feel—even better than them." Sparky shoots Charlie a puzzled look as all the Auts nod, muttering to themselves.

"In RW, emotions and senses are considered the most important strengths. They keep the peace among all people and animals. Up there, difference is admired, not put up with."

The Auts gaze at each other and sigh. Sparkles shrugs. "But our gifts are too uncontrollable to be useful to anyone."

Moojag paces through the crowd. "I've been there, seen it—RW."

"You, Moojag?" asks Sparkles. "How?" The Auts glare at him as he hops over to Charlie and lingers beside her.

"He's been helping us with a special mission," she explains. "He brought us these three Real Worlders to help get you out of here, if you want it."

As the Auts scan the room for said Real Worlders, Sparky points to the floor and presses his fingertips together in the shape of a sloping roof.

"Of course you've come to know Gajoomdom as home," says Charlie, "but above ground you'd be free to be yourselves and do what makes you truly happy. You'd be among people who respect you for *you*."

Sparkles crosses her arms. "You can't just decide to be happy."

Charlie smiles at her and points to the banner on the wall. "You certainly can, and you've had that message in front of you all along."

ONE WHO CONTROLS OTHERS MAY BE POWERFUL, BUT ONE WHO HAS MASTERED THEMSELF IS MIGHTIER STILL –Tao Te Ching

"Yes, the Conqip are powerful," she continues, "but they do not control you—not really." The Auts slump, shaking their heads. "You just have to believe in yourself."

Sparky perks up, charged by the idea that he could actually be liked, that someone might just appreciate, even love, his uniqueness. Somehow he always knew he was special, but his overreaction to the smallest problems—even his biggest achievements—made him feel stupid or weird. He never thought he was worth anything until this impossible moment.

Sparkles squints at Charlie and crosses her arms. "How do we know this ain't a trick?"

"Should we take off our Gajoom skins now?" Nema whispers. Charlie nods.

The Auts gasp as Nema draws up her stripy tube. Slowly, she reveals her glistening feet, dulled silver-skin-covered body and flushed sun-kissed face. Squinting in the bright artificial light, she drops the tube and untangles her long ebony hair.

Adam and Izzy whip off theirs, too. "We didn't know you existed," Izzy tells them, her clasped hands mirroring Moojag's.

Sparkles grunts, peering at the peculiar looking visitors, and takes Sparky's hand firmly in hers. "Sounds about right. Why *them*, though? They look odd."

"They're here," explains Charlie, "because they come from the same generation of Auts as you."

Sparkles approaches Izzy and runs her fingers over PIE's smooth hexagonal cells. "Family?"

"You could say so, yes."

Sparky checks out Nema's Spondylux. "High- or low-functioning?" asks Sparkles.

"What?" asks Adam.

Sparkles nods to her brother, his finger pointed up in the air.

"We don't use labels in RW," says Adam.

"Pardon?"

"We would never judge *anyone*," says Nema.

"Dividing people," Adam explains, "only causes hate and fear. And anyway, we're all equally useful."

Sparky leans in to sniff Adam's skin. "Everyone's the same?" asks Sparkles, pulling her brother off him.

"We treat each other the same, and we all wear PIE, but every person is different and unique in their own way." Sparky snorts uncontrollably as he imagines a perfect world full of strange looking lizard people covered in cherry pie.

"It's the only way for peace," says Izzy, stretching her PIE away from her clammy real skin.

Sparkles turns and looks into the distance to process the alien words. "And what do you do there? What would *we* do there?"

"Whatever you want," answers Adam, "and you'll get all the time you need to figure it out."

"*Takiwātanga*," mutters Sparky. He pictures a lab full of Auts on smartphones, surrounded by numberless clocks.

"Even if it takes our entire lives?" asks Sparkles.

"Maybe, but you'll have to make yourself useful in the meantime."

Sparkles sighs. "Useful? We're pretty useless."

Sparky looks down with clenched fists.

"No way," says Izzy. "Neurodivergents help others to see."

"Huh?"

"Because we see things differently," explains Nema. "We notice things others miss. Neurodivergents have always created stuff that others could never even dream up themselves, like your Gajoomstiks."

"But the Conqip said—"

"Forget the Conqip," says Adam.

"They said we're only good for coding," calls another Aut, "and we're lucky to have work at all."

"You're great at this stuff, of course," says Charlie, "but that's only *one* of the things you're remarkable at."

"I *knew* it," cries Sparkles. "They lied, AGAIN!"

"I'm afraid they've lied to us all. But now you can finally

make your own informed choice. In the end, you must do what is right for *you*." An eerie silence fills the bleak lab. The confused Auts have never had to make a decision on their own. They've never been allowed; never imagined they could.

Charlie steps closer to the agitated crowd. "Before you decide if you want to go, we will need your help to apply the Auticode to the Gajooms. Once completed, we'll get you straight up to the Real World."

"Auticode?" whispers one of the Auts.

"The antidote to the last phase of coding on the Gajooms," explains Charlie. "We discovered the Conqip have been using the code to turn the Gajooms nasty. They're plotting to take over the Real World."

"The codes we created to multiply the Gajooms," Sparkles explains to her fellow Auts. "But it's not OUR fault," she adds, seeing Sparky's eyes well up.

"No, it absolutely is *not* your doing," says Charlie. "The Conqip have taken advantage of your honest and loyal nature; abused your trust to feed their greed. This time they've gone too far."

Sparkles and Sparky peer round at the other workers and turn back, giving Charlie a nod. "Okay, we'll help you."

Charlie clasps her hands and ushers the siblings over

to the mount of liquorice strips. "The RWs have already deciphered the Auticode, which Moojag has triggered into this run of strips. We must wrap the Gajooms, right away."

The Auts dither for a moment, muttering among themselves before dismounting their balls. They stagger over to the pile, whispering as they lurch past the Real Worlders.

Charlie whirls one of the strips in the air like a lasso. She seizes the Gajoom beside her, spins it round twice and bandages it in the strip as it turns, until it's completely wrapped in a spiralling stripe. "So," she says, letting the giddy Gajoom flop down and bounce away. "Are we doing this? Are we going to beat the conniving Conqip together?"

They all shuffle closer and glance at one another before finally calling out a fist-pumping, harmonious "YES!"

Charlie wields another strip. "Then GO STRIPE!"

All twenty-one Auts charge at the throbbing pile, gathering up a strip and making for their unsuspecting Gajooms.

Sparky grimaces, straddling a candy robot twice his size.

"Hold it down!" cries Sparkles, pinning her sticky captive to the ground.

One by one, the Gajooms are rolled in the strips until they're completely covered in haphazard, purple spirals. "Wonderful, Auts," calls Charlie. "Don't forget to release them."

Once striped, the Gajooms bolt up into their usual perpendicular selves, leaving their tacky trails across the lab floor and all over the over-excited Auts. Nema grabs two strips from the dwindling pile and hands one to Izzy. She hunts for some slightly smaller sticks among the battling throng of Auts and Gajooms.

Izzy points to a jittery pair in the corner, "There, let's try *them*." She and Nema sprint over, but the Gajooms leap back. Each time the girls move in, the Gajooms hop away.

"Slowly," whispers Sparkles, "they sense you coming."

Clever candy. The Auts must have designed the Gajooms to be like them. And the Gajoom skin probably has sensory cells just like PIE, so they can tell when something's coming.

Nema grabs Izzy's shoulder and presses a finger to her lips. She signals to the sticks and edges forward. She sneaks up and pounces on the first Gajoom, but it slithers right through her hooped arms.

"NUMB SPOT," Sparkles yells over.

Izzy glares at the Aut. "She's got a nerve..."

"Not *you*—" says Nema, "the Gajoom."

"You gotta grab 'em in the numb spot," calls Adam, "right in their middle, and then pin 'em down."

Izzy creeps with Nema over to the Gajooms. "Isn't that what pre-Surgers called peaceful people?"

"Nah, that was numb *skull*."

Izzy pounces on the thick stick, clamping herself to its middle. But the Gajoom narrows itself to slip through her grip. She huffs and turns to check on Nema, who's bent over giggling at Adam. He has somehow pinned down two Gajooms and is wrestling them both between his arms and legs. Izzy flings her strip over him and starts wrapping one of the sticks. Nema leaps over to wrap the other one.

"WATCH it," calls Adam, with Izzy taping his face to a Gajoom. She shakes her head at Nema, still giggling, and rips off the strip like a pre-Surge plaster. "OUCH!" They release the Gajooms, letting Adam flop to the floor, and watch them bounce back up before bounding off to the side.

"Right," says Charlie, "think that's your lot." She plucks the purple floss from her hair and rubs it off onto her handkerchief. "Sparkles and Sparky, it's time to return them to the factory."

"Oh, *woman*."

Charlie raises a brow at Sparkles. "We must clear them out quickly, and you're the best with them, so—" Sparky scrambles over and tugs the hem of her jacket, pointing his trembling finger at three shadows looming in the triangular passage. "QUICK—tidy the Gajooms."

The Auts scurry to organise the sticks, while the RWs

wriggle into their disguises and blend into the Gajoom mob. The Conqip leaders barge into the lab, throwing down their champagne flutes as they enter. Brix smirks at the Auts jumping from the ear-splitting sound of shattering glass.

Travis claps his hands in the face of an Aut shielding herself from the bouncing shards. "CLEAR IT UP!" he shouts, poking her shoulder.

"Liquorice feed over yet?" Aldon asks Charlie.

"Yes, A. They're just being returned to the factory."

The man raises his hollow cheeks in a squint to scan the unevenly bandaged sticks and points to Nema, Izzy, and Adam. "Tell me, woman, what indeed is the matter with *those*? They appear not to have been fed."

"Ah…they…weren't hungry." Izzy's stomach quietly growls at the thought of Charlie's crazy idea.

Travis closes in on them. "Looks like the boorish imbeciles that brought us our sweets, no?"

"Never mind them," says Aldon. "Charlie, see that they are fed forthwith. Now, what progress with the code?"

Charlie turns, dodging his glare. "Of course, A. We're working on it."

"I see." Aldon scowls at the trembling teens. "No need to look so stunned; you just carry on doing your thing for your Conqip, and watch our names go down in history."

Travis gawks at the Auts shuffling back to their stations, heads bent. "What on earth is wrong with the idiots now?"

"Who knows," answers Brix, smirking. "Perfect moment for a spot of betting, no?"

"Oh, marvellous. Lucky dip?"

"Of course."

Travis closes his eyes, spins round twice, and extends his arm out to point blind.

Brix grins at the target. "Perfecto." They exchange a wink and strut up to Sparky.

"But the scraggy mute won't utter a single word," says Travis.

Brix sniggers. "You underestimate the Aut so. I say at least *one* utterance will spout from the freak."

"Hey, SPARKS."

Silence...

"Oi! *You*! MORON...Travis is talking to you."

Silence...

"Say something," Sparkles whispers under her breath, "*anything*."

Sparky's throat swells and face reddens as he tries to unscramble the words filling his head. He finally opens his mouth to spit one out. The word, as clear as code, just freezes on the tip of his tongue, with beads of sweat emerging from his forehead.

"Look what you've done, Travis," says Brix.

Travis scoffs. "Me? Nah. Scrawny does it all by himself."

Brix dips a hand into his trouser pocket and pulls out a pair of razor sharp scissors. "Give it a minute." He waves the blades like a crazed windshield wiper in front of Sparky's face.

"ARRGGGHH..." screams Sparky, erupting like a volcano spewing all its pent-up fury. Unable to take any more, Sparky lashes out at the tyrant, kicking and punching him.

"I WIN," calls Brix, grimacing as he tackles the uncontrollable Aut.

"Hang on," says Travis, "'arrggghh' is never a word."

"Of course it is," says Brix, gagging at the sight of Sparky retching over a pool of vomit. "It's a response at any rate."

Travis covers his nose from the stench and darts to the mirrored door to check his hair. "Fair enough, Brix," he says, rolling his eyes and striding over to Aldon. "I'll give you this one."

"Enough of your silly antics," huffs Aldon. "Leave them to get on with their job. Don't see why you waste your energy on this anti-social lot, especially since there's a Pof contest on." His minions' faces light up.

"Enjoy," calls Charlie, gritting her teeth and tightening a fist behind her back as they head for the door. Aldon waves his hand in the air, belting Travis' head with it on their way out.

***

"You okay, Sparky?" Izzy asks, crouching beside the Aut as everyone gathers round.

"Not so much," answers Sparkles, patting her brother's shoulder.

Nema wipes away the tears rolling down her cheeks. "You don't have to put up with them for much longer."

"That's right," says Charlie, offering Sparky a comforting arm and looking to the others. "It's time for you to decide what you want to do with your future. It's here, and it's in your hands, my dear Auts."

They peer down, shaking their heads, and gaze back over at the big banner:

...ONE WHO HAS MASTERED THEMSELF IS MIGHTIER STILL

They all turn and nod, an unspoken pact to start their new life in the Real World.

28

ABOUT THE POF

The Auts guide the Gajooms to the chute and watch them zoom back over to the factory. Charlie places a hand on her chest. "We are fortunate. It appears Poof Poof still hasn't told the Conqip. There's a good chance we can win the Pofs over, too."

"Shouldn't we get the Auts out," asks Adam, "before there's any trouble?"

"They need more time to process this big change in their lives. If we try to take them now, they'll panic and just stick with what they know."

"As soon as the Conqip discover the Auts gone," adds Biermont, "the Pofs will be blamed and all chances of them leaving too will be lost. They're physically and mentally strong, but emotionally very weak."

"Once we leave, there will be no return," says Charlie.

"It's too risky. And who'll make the Pofs see the Conqip for the bullies they are?"

Nema wonders why the Pofs don't get how bad the Conqip really are. *Maybe the Pofs think they owe the Conqip for saving them when their parents couldn't cope.*

"The original Pofs," explains Charlie, "were the girls your grandmother spoke of in her message. They were involved in experiments by Zizanth, scientists who claimed to have found a cure for every disorder by mutating cicada memory cells with a humans'."

Izzy gasps and turns to Nema, appropriately bug-eyed. "They're the ones that live for years underground," she whispers. "And then, when they finally come out all together, the buzzing…it's TORTURE!" Adam gives his fired-up friend a gentle nudge. "Sorry," she whispers, "no PIE—no warnings."

"At first, the experiments were successful," Charlie continues, smiling softly at Izzy. "The children became super strong. This delighted everybody, of course, but then the children sprouted wings, stopped growing, and became uncontrollably over-excitable. In order to hide the results of their failure, Zizanth forced the parents to give up their children to the Conqip. This is why they are so very vulnerable."

"But wasn't that a boy back at the Palace?" asks Nema.

Charlie looks down at her velvet pumps and sighs. "He is half Pof, one of many born down here. You may have noticed their smaller wings."

Nema doesn't recognise the feelings racing through her right now with no PIE to explain it. But somehow, she knows that the wicked Conqip are behind Charlie's weird silence and the sadness in her eyes.

"And the magic?" asks Izzy.

Charlie's shoulders relax and her worn face breaks into a smile, as though a weight has lifted with the change of subject. "Ah, that's not actually magic, simply a shrewd visual trick to steal your attention. They were homesick for too long, and fantasy has become their sort of therapy. They're masters at creating illusion, conjuring what they love."

"Food?" asks Izzy, picturing Poof Poof's glistening toffee popcorn tree.

"Yes, especially candy. They've learned to use food to feel safe. That's why they'll do almost anything to get it."

"You must hurry," says Biermont, "if you're to convince Poof Poof, too."

Charlie turns back to the anxious crowd. "Dear Auts, you have three hours to prepare."

"15:26?" yells one. The Aut paces behind her station, staring up at the clock to sync it with her smartwatch. "15:26 and 14 seconds."

"Yes, fine. And you'll be permitted to take with you one special object. It must be small enough to grasp. There won't be anyone to carry things for you." Charlie raises a hand. "No computers." The Auts scowl at her cold words and gaze miserably at their PCs and Macs. "Nor clothes." Moojag glares at her, crossing his legs and clutching the letters of his hat. "But when we reach the other side, you'll be the proud new owners of PIE." Charlie turns to the RWs and pinches Adam. "And *you* guys, no longer need these Gajoom skins."

The Auts screw up their faces and glance at Izzy. She's already shuffled out the disguise and is stretching her turquoise arms and legs. They gaze back up at the banner and hunch their shoulders with a drawn out sigh.

"We better get them out quick," says Izzy, watching Moojag. Head bowed and mumbling numbers to himself. "They could be changing their minds already."

"*Ichi...zwei...tria...quattro...beş...*"

"What's Moojag doing with his hands?" Izzy asks.

Nema follows him trace a curly six in the air. "He's drawing numbers."

"He always counts when he's nervous," explains Charlie. "Helps regulate emotion."

"Very calming," says Adam, rotating his arm in a figure of eight.

Moojag drops his hands in a huff and locks them behind his back. "*S'il vous plait,* mock me not. Mock me. Mock me not..."

Nema shakes her head. "We weren't making fun, honest. We just wouldn't. Stimming is the best."

Izzy nods, keeps on nodding. Adam smirks, raising his hands to steady Izzy's dizzy head. "Back to the switching room then?" he says, peering round. Moojag realigns his hat and mopes over to door K.

Izzy squints at Charlie stepping into the hexagonal room. "But won't the Conqip be there?"

"In the audience, yes, but the Pofs will be backstage."

"Good luck," calls Biermont, standing back with the Auts.

Adam pokes his head back into the lab. "You'll come up with us though?"

"Not today."

"Moojag?" asks Nema, popping her head out too. But my boy just twitches his mouth and shakes his head. Izzy pulls Nema and Adam back into the switching room and they chase after Charlie through door T42.

"We must find Kitty," Charlie calls. "She's our only hope of getting through to Poof Poof."

Izzy bends down to swipe some floss from the ground. "Don't eat the floor," says Nema. "Or the ceiling."

My girl wonders what Moojag must be feeling. And what Real Worlders will think when they find out what I did.

"We should eat something real soon," says Izzy.

"And *real*," adds Nema.

"That's what I said."

"No, you didn't."

"Something REAL soon."

"She did," says Adam as they approach a high, glass-bricked wall by the Palace gates. "And yeah, we should! Real *and* real soon."

29

POF STARS & THE MARSHMALLOW CHAMBER

"Welcome to POF STARS," announces a Pof. She flutters her peach-tinted wings behind a screen in the wall at the theatre gates. "Passes, please."

Charlie flashes her Conqip badge. "My dear, we are here to see Poof Poof. Kindly let us through."

"Other passes, please."

Charlie presents her ID again. The agitated attendant tuts at her, jabbing a notice on the wall of her little booth with her wand. She squints at the unfamiliar characters lingering behind Charlie. "You *know* I *know,* you *know* I *know* you *know*—no passes equals no entry."

Charlie peers through the window and spots a trail of yellow marshmallow on the ground. Inside the drawer beside the girl, a small chunk of it is nestled in a pile of torn up papers. "I hear you are particularly fond of yellow marshmallow?"

"Yes, pineapple. My favourite."

Charlie eyes the name tag pinned to the girl's yellow vest. "Excellent choice, *Deja*. Yellow is my favourite colour too. You know, I've never tried pineapple. I wonder if I could have a little try?"

Deja squints at her and looks down at the drawer as Charlie quickly turns to the RWs and rubs her ear. "What are *they* doing here?" she asks, sifting through the drawer's contents.

"Oh, they're just my helpers," answers Charlie, secretly waving them on. They crouch down and creep under the barrier as Deja tweezes out the sole piece of marshmallow. She prises off a measly corner, stuffs the bigger portion in her mouth, and hands over the tiny piece.

Charlie pops the morsel on her tongue. "Mmmm, it's *so* good. How decent of you to share your LAST piece." Deja's face drops as she gulps the final bite. Charlie points to a big glistening mound of marshmallow just dumped by two Pofs. "But look at that mountain of joy over there!"

Deja's eyes light up. She spins round, scrambles down, and reappears crouching by the pile. Charlie quickly crawls under the barrier and sprints to the others as Deja scoops marshmallows.

"Well done, friends," says Charlie, joining the others.

"No *problemo*," Adam answers, bowing his head.

"Come on," says Charlie, noticing Deja careen back to her booth. "This way." They bolt after her to the backstage entrance of the glass-domed theatre and enter through the open door. The Pofs are buzzing around, rehearsing their acts.

"This is a strictly POF zone!" shouts a screechy voice.

"Poof Poof," calls Charlie, glancing back wide-eyed at the friends. Nema ogles Adam and glares back at Izzy squirming behind her.

"Who are these creatures? They are not Pofs! Neither are they Gajooms…and definitely *not* Conqip."

"They are with *me*."

"I can see that, darling. What are they doing *here* on our grounds—in Gajoomdom?!"

"They've come from RW to help us stop the Gajooms from destroying their world," Charlie whispers. "We can all finally be free of the Conqip."

"How dare you speak so wickedly of our saviours." Poof Poof scowls at the three friends. "And as for impersonating Gajooms 9, 8, and 4… Yes, I *know* what you've been up to. Horrendous behaviour."

"Do you trust the Conqip?" Charlie asks her. "Have they

kept their word, looked after you the way they promised to?"

"We live comfortably enough. All the sweets we desire—eternity of pleasure."

"Perhaps," adds Charlie, "but at what cost? And they trample on the sweet Pofs' kindnesses without a care."

Poof Poof bumps past Charlie, cracking back her wings in a red-faced rage. "Ungrateful creature."

"Sure, you're provided for," Charlie calls after her, "but are you truly healthy and happy?"

"*Never* been happier." Charlie frowns as the Pof hovers backwards for the stage. "I'll deal with this in a minute... Don't you *dare* move!" Poof Poof shouts back. She peers through the curtains at Kitty singing in the pink spotlight, and calls, "Come on darling, hurry up!" She swoops on stage, flapping her wings at her daughter. Kitty bows and squints through the glare at the clapping audience, before zooming off between the curtains.

"Hello, Kitty," says Charlie as a grinning Kitty crashes into her. "Come with us to the Real World."

"Get my power first. Go anywhere I like."

Charlie shakes her head. "That won't get you out of Gajoomdom. But we can get you out. All the Pofs, if they want it."

Kitty eyes the strangers' metallic skins. "Dorothy?"

"That film is so *old* world," says Izzy.

"We have actors too," says Nema, stepping in front of her pouty friend. "You'll love them even more. And we have story tellers—"

Kitty's wings perk up. "Are *you* from Real World?"

Adam nods. "Free to go anywhere and be whoever we want."

"Me too?"

"Of course," says Charlie, "and your mum, and all your friends."

"Friend?" Kitty asks, gazing round.

"We can be friends, if you like," says Nema.

"Do you have sweets?"

"Not exactly," says Adam.

"You'll love our avocado ice-cream," says Nema.

Izzy pokes Kitty's sagging wing. "It's really good, honest."

"And our lush mangoes," adds Adam. "Tangy blackberries, too. All *real*." Kitty's face lights up again, her wings fluttering as she rubs her hands together.

"But first we have to convince Poof Poof and the others," explains Charlie.

"Mummy don't like Real World. People not nice."

The girls glance at each other, shaking their heads. "*Super* nice," says Izzy. "We're from there. You like *us*, don't you?"

Kitty turns away, peeking at them from the corner of her eye. "You take our power and fruit."

Charlie bends over to prop up Kitty's wings. "I'm afraid the Conqip have lied about many things, my dear Pof. There has never been any real fruit here." Kitty shakes her head. "I'm afraid so. Our food is only flavoured to taste like the real thing."

"RW has only ever had *real* fruit," says Adam. "Vegetables, too. I know because we grow them ourselves."

"What? *Balls*?"

"*Ve-ge-ta-ble*," says Izzy.

"Like fruit but not as sweet," explains Nema.

"Not-sweet fruit?"

"Juicy tomatoes and golden peppers are the sweetest. Technically they *are* fruit."

"Because they have seeds," Adam explains, "and are from a bush, not underground. Cucumbers, too."

Kitty mutters to herself, gazing at the floor. "What? From the ground. Yuck."

"They're tasty," adds Charlie, "and full of good stuff."

"Power?"

"A tonne!"

Nema crouches down to show Kitty her conked Spondylux. "You can use this to watch movies and learn about anything you want."

Kitty strokes the shell. "Film I like—*there*?"

"Sure, as long as PIE says it's safe."

"Pie? I like pie. We go *now*?"

"First, Kitty," says Charlie, clasping her hands, "we need you to persuade mum to come too." The Pof hangs her head. "Can you try? *Please*?"

"Okay…" she says, moping off, "get my power first."

"No! Wait—" Kitty zooms back through the curtains.

Izzy sighs. "Will we *ever* get home?"

"DON'T YOU BET ON IT!" screams Poof Poof, barging toward them with a dozen jittery Pofs ferrying an enormous net.

"Go!" Charlie shouts to my girl and her friends. But the webbing drops down, trapping them all beneath it. The Pofs whizz round, weaving ropes though the holes in the net and yanking them tight.

"TRAITOR!" cries Poof Poof, watching the huge sagging bundle get dragged across the stage and hauled into the air.

Charlie sighs. "The Conqip must know."

Izzy gasps, hooking her fingers through the net. Nema squeezes her eyes shut as they swoop over the stage. The bundle skims the audience of puffed-up Conqip and tickled Pofs as they're whisked out of the dome, through the gates,

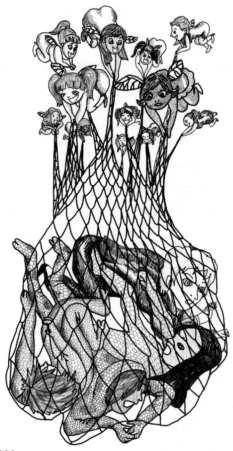

and into the Palace.

The charged Pofs lug them down a dingy corridor and release them through the open hatch in the floor into a steamy, dark chamber. They cackle as the RWs plunge with Charlie into a warm, pink, squidgy substance. Adam springs back up, spitting out the marshmallowy gunk, as Izzy ducks her head back in.

Nema never liked getting dirty. As a kid she never made a mess or touched stuff. *This marshmallow stuff looked tasty*, she thinks, *before those dodgy bubbles started rising from the surface and going pop. PIE would be flashing orange right now. At least Izzy's farts don't smell.*

CLUNK!

"Uh oh," whispers Adam, cocking his head.

"WHAT?" Izzy blurts.

"We're locked in," calls Nema.

"They appear to have taken us hostage," says Charlie.

"I'm *never* getting out of here now," says Izzy, shovelling handfuls of the gooey marshmallow into her mouth.

Nema gawks at her. "Stop eating and chill. We don't need to go any lower, or we're definitely not getting out of here."

Charlie draws up her arms. "Just keep your head and hands out of the stuff."

Nema starts to count, "One, two, three—"

"FOOLS," a tinny voice screeches through the creaking hatch. "We'll never leave our sweet life for the grotty *real* world."

Nema sputters, with the sticky stuff seeping into her mouth, as Adam points to a metal grille in the ceiling. "It's that purple-winged snitch," Izzy sighs. "And we're sinking, by the way."

30

WINGING IT

"DISOBEY and pay the price," Aldon shouts at the Auts after firing a string of insults from his trembling, machine-gun mouth. The furious man grabs Sparkles' arm. The nervy workers glare at each other and gaze at the banner above their friend's head as he pins her to the wall. "LOOK AT ME, Auts, when I address you."

Brix sneers at them. "Up *here*," he says, tapping his eye.

"A couple of matchsticks, perhaps," suggests Travis, "to prop the lids open?"

"You're such a quack."

Aldon releases Sparkles to slap Travis and Brix's heads at once. "Point is, you punks, one of these geeks is an imposter." He jabs his walking stick in the direction of the stumped workers. "Among you lurks a conspirator working against Gajoomdom."

The Auts gulp, trapped in their petrified bodies, as Brix spies Sparky glaring at the wall. "YOU!" Sparky mutters something, barely raising his head. "I *beg* your pardon?"

"Yes, BOY," yells Travis. "SPEAK UP."

"*NO!*"

"Misery Guts spoke an actual word!" calls Brix. "It's a bloody miracle."

"Looks like I win *this* one, Brixy," Travis says, grinning.

Aldon scans the room with his finger. "So, which one of you weasels *has* been messing with the code?"

"We know what you've been up to," says Brix, "colluding with lesser beings of the old world."

Aldon stamps his foot forward. "Only an ungrateful Aut could be so despicably vile. YOU!" he blares, turning to Moojag and striking the floor with his cane.

"*Moi?*"

"Yes, *monsieur, TOI!*"

"It's disgusting," grunts Travis.

"What's the matter with it?" asks Brix. "Finally get the mute to speak, and it's in a bloody different language."

Aldon smirks, pacing round Moojag and jabbing him hard between the shoulder blades. "It's French. But that's not *all* that's wrong with the little freak."

Brix and Travis circle the boy, fondling the velvety soft

arms of his suit as they probe his body for clues.

"*Aha*, what's this?" pipes Brix, ripping off the jacket. "Well, well, it's all dressed up like a POF." The Auts gasp, clenching their teeth and wincing. "NO, they can't be!" he cries, failing to rip off Moojag's delicate wings. "He's not *wearing* them, Travis! They're bloody REAL."

Aldon raises a wiry brow. "Lads, we appear to have found our culprit."

Moojag clasps his hands, letting his exposed mangled wings flop down. "*S'il vous plaît*, don't hurt my friends."

Brix cackles. "Since when do Auts have friends?"

"I believe," says Aldon, "he's referring to our visitors from RW."

"Oh, *them*."

"You're missing the point," says Travis. "He's not exactly an Aut, now, is he."

"He's a MUTANT one," blares Brix.

Moojag bows his head, "*Vraiment*."

"What's the little git saying now?" asks Travis.

"Talk in English," says Brix, "like the rest of us."

Moojag sighs. "It's true."

"Wasn't so hard, was it?"

"What shall we do with him?" Travis asks, coughing into his hand and smearing slimy phlegm across Moojag's cheek.

Aldon grimaces at the boy's mucused face. "You understand, master Moojag—you're a Pof. Your place is with *them* now; no longer in here with the Auts."

Moojag bows his head. "*Compris.*"

"Pardon?"

"I understand." *I understand how I am different,* my boy thinks to himself, *why I never fit in with the other Auts. Aldon is right; I don't belong here anymore. But if I don't belong here—where DO I belong? How will I fit in with the Pofs? Or should I be with my 'real' family in RW? But I'm stuck here now anyhow…*

"Back to your stations, Auts," shouts Brix. "And back to work, you lazy good-for-nothing nerds."

Travis tugs Moojag's wing. "This way, *Buzby.*"

"Yes, come along," says Aldon. "You don't want to miss the private show Poof Poof has put on with the interfering 'real world' nerds." Moojag lowers his head, as a sullen Sparky and sorrowful Sparkles wave goodbye. "A delightful opportunity for you to say *au revoir* to your accomplices."

"*Mais, non,*" whimpers Moojag.

"*Mais,* YES."

The Conqip stride out of the lab, cackling like crows. Moojag, lagging behind, turns to wave his friends goodbye and follows after Brix into the switching room.

"Aren't you curious *why* the freak has wings?" Aldon asks the men. They stall in the doorway, returning frenzied nods as he veers left towards door T42. "There was a rumour that the very first Zizanth experiment was on an autistic boy, *not* a girl." The men's jaws drop. "And it was on the grandson of the Conqip who went Real World on us."

"NO! *Who*?" asks Travis. "Not—Nem Avti?"

"Quite. The treatment failed, you see, and the boy turned out slower and more peculiar than before." Moojag stops cold in his tracks.

Brix sneers back at him. "NO—you mean *Buzby* here?"

"Someone must've sneaked him in with the Auts," says Travis.

"Apparently so."

Brix glances at my wide-eyed, snivelling Moojag. "You look like you've been hit by a truck, Buzby."

My boy doesn't understand the horrendous man's comment or what it means, but he's sure it is *mean*. The homonym makes him smile. He loves words that are spelled and sound the same but have different meanings. *Mean*. For a moment, he feels normal again. Whatever *that* is.

"And the girls?" asks Brix.

"The next to be treated was indeed a girl. She could barely walk when she arrived at the clinic in her wheelchair.

She was cured and became super strong, so they continued only treating girls with learning difficulties but who also had a physical disability. Syndrome this, syndrome that— you name it, they were experimenting on it. Trouble came months later when they all started sprouting bloody wings. And they stopped growing too."

Travis glares back at Moojag. "What are you saying, A? The weirdo Pofs weren't *meant* to have wings?"

"Of course not, moron. What? You think the reprobates *asked* for it? 'And while you're at it, grow my kid a pair of wings'."

"They wouldn't have lasted a second in the old world with wings," says Brix, whacking Travis in the back. "Isn't that why *we* got lumbered with the brats in the first place?"

As Moojag drags behind them into the Palace, he recalls his hazy memories of the old world: People wading past them through the water on route to the clinic with his gran; me, tearfully waving goodbye. The reeking disinfectant, the frosted windows. Clinging to the back of the van with the other Auts in the dark. Gazing up at the moon for the last time before Biermont closed the lighthouse door behind them. And all this time...believing he was an Aut.

But you see, my boy has always felt different. He just never understood how or why. As much as he tried to hide his wings and be like the others, somehow he never managed to fit in. Now he learns that he's the only SuperAut with wings and that they grew out of some experiment. And, one of the very RWs he brought here to save them all is likely his sister. Moojag barely recognises himself anymore, or the beautiful, amazing body he's in.

"Oi, *Buzby*," Travis snorts, directing him to the end of the dark corridor. "You're a POF boy! That's why you're so bloody short."

"Always thought he looked like the winged freaks," says Brix. He blindly punches behind himself and wallops my boy to the ground. I drop beside him and blow a kiss. He senses my breath sweep his cheek like a soft, cool breeze and, for a moment, it soothes the pain.

Aldon stamps on the circular hatch in the concrete floor, making Moojag jolt. "Ready to meet some dinosaurs?" He unhooks a megaphone from the wall and crouches over the grille. "Greetings."

"Help," mumbles Izzy, almost up to her eyeballs in gloopy marshmallow.

"I hear these trespassers attempted to abduct our citizens?"

"A misunderstanding," Charlie calls up.

"Charlie? Disappointed in *you*."

Brix nods. "Be-tray-al, young lady."

"Great pity," says Travis, shaking his head, "to lose one of our finest."

"The Auts deserve more," calls Charlie. "Time to let them go—"

"They *ought* to know better," cackles Brix. "As for this one…" he says, jabbing Moojag in the chest to knock him back down, "I suppose you knew all about the Aut-Pof?"

"Don't hurt him," says Charlie. "It's not his fault."

"Probably *her*," whispers Travis, "who sneaked him in with the Auts."

"Who cares," says Aldon, glaring at Moojag as he kicks him in the shin. "Why are *you* still here? Quit fidgeting and clear off." Brix growls, slamming down the hatch with his foot, as Moojag limps away drawing shapes in the air.

***

Adam frowns at Charlie. "Buzby?"

"They must have found out."

"What?"

"Moojag…you see, he's a Pof…" Izzy croaks between gulps of marshmallow.

"How did he end up with the Auts?" asks Nema.

"He's both *Aut* and *Pof.* Long story, my friends."

"I don't see us getting out of here any time soon, do *you*?"

Izzy chuckles. "So that's how he hovers."

Nema glances at her friends. "Don't you see? Moojag isn't *just* an Aut and a Pof. He's my brother."

"Monzi?" asks Adam. "*That's* why he was so upset at your Gran's Hola."

"Yes, Gran is his gran too. But that also means it was Gran, and probably mum as well, who gave him away to the nasty Conqip."

"I knew it," says Izzy. "You two look exactly the same."

"And the woman I saw," Nema adds, "was my mum."

"Well," says Charlie, "dear Moojag will need more persuading than the others if he's now realised he's a Pof too."

"He won't want to leave them behind, will he?" asks Nema.

Charlie sighs. "No, he likely won't, because he's so loyal. But he'll also feel a duty to go home. His heart will be torn."

"It'll be okay..." says Adam.

"Hey," mumbles Izzy, "you reckon we could eat our way out of this mess?"

Nema shakes her marshmallow-coated head. "Not one of your better ideas, girl."

31

MACARON BRIBE

My flustered Aut-Pof zigzags into the factory, stumbling straight into Biermont and propping up his hat. "There you are, Monty."

"The Conqips stormed the lab again, so I shot back over."

"No time to lose," says Moojag. "They're in the marshmallow—"

"What?"

"Not Wats, Charlie and the RWs." Moojag hunches over and rubs his tender chest. "Poof Poof snitched." He lowers his jacket and turns to reveal his wings. "And they've seen these..."

"I know, Moojag. We've known all along." My boy looks up with sad eyes and shakes his head. "Your grandmother was a Conqip. She secretly put you in with the Auts to protect your true identity, to keep you safe." Moojag's shoulders sag, letting his heavy head drop between them. "She didn't want you to be treated differently."

My boy slips the jacket back over his wings. "But I have always been different."

"She thought she was doing the best for you. It was a terrible time before the Surge."

"And Nema—she is my sister, *oui*?"

"It would seem so. Your grandmother was incredibly good at keeping secrets."

Moojag hasn't the words to express his feelings right now, but he knows he has to move fast. "We must help her and her friends before it's too late. But they are in the chamber and the hatch is locked!"

"Only a Pof can unlock it," says Biermont. "Maybe Kitty can help us. She must still be in the theatre."

Moojag hovers over to the assembly line. "It will take our top candy to convince her."

"Well, what have we got?"

Moojag presses his hands together and makes for the Gajooms' sweetest, most awesome treat: the Golden Macaron Tower. Biermont arches over the conveyor, allowing the enormous cone-shaped tower of purple, gold-leafed macarons to ride up onto his sticky Gajoom-skin back.

"How sorry I feel for those snails," says Moojag, watching

Biermont swagger under the monument, "carrying their houses on their backs their entire lives."

Biermont grins as he prepares to leap off. "Lucky snail with a house like this one, though, eh?"

"But *imagine*, Monty, if he were forced to eat his own roof! He should finish up *absolument* homeless." Moojag hovers out after Biermont through door K, into the switching room, and straight out T42. Barely touching the winding peach-pebbled path, they bolt through the candy haze and head to the theatre.

***

"Welcome to Pof Stars," mutters a drowsy Deja, humped over in her booth. "Passes, please."

Moojag presents his ID and flashes a forced smile, mirroring the image in his photo. "G21 and I are delivering the winning prize to Kitty."

Deja presses her nose up against the screen to assess the glittering, multi-tiered object on Biermont's back. "What is that?"

Moojag curtsies. "*Macaron Tour D'Or*."

"Can I try?"

"*Sûr* —if you let us deliver in person, I will allow you to swipe a macaron."

Deja flings up the screen, pokes her head through, and reaches out to tease a cookie. She pops it in her mouth, fluttering her eyes as she buzzes Moojag and G21 through the barrier. Gently pressing a finger to her lips, she crushes the crispy shell with her tongue and sucks out the fluffy, liquorice-infused cream. Moojag zooms over to the glass dome and crouches in front of the solitary Pof sitting cross-legged on the ground.

"Busy now—"

"But it's Charlie."

Kitty squints at him and over at G21.

"Poof Poof has thrown her and the RWs into the chamber."

Kitty gazes at the tower. "It's your prize," says Moojag.

She raises the glistening medal hanging from her neck. "Go anywhere I like now."

"Yes, but this is your *other* prize," he explains, teetering as he detaches the giant showstopper from Biermont.

Kitty jumps up, clasping her clammy hands. "COOKIES!"

"First," says Moojag, wiggling a finger, "you must do a job for us."

"What?"

"You must help us free Charlie and our friends."

Kitty crosses her arms. "Poof Poof said they lie."

"False," says Moojag, rocking his head. "They're helping

the Auts and Pofs escape to RW."

"That's what Charlie said."

"She is correct," says Moojag, lightly patting Kitty's shoulder. "*Vraiment.*"

"Take cookie?"

"Of course, we will even carry it for you." Moojag turns to Biermont, winking at the ex-Conqip reluctantly bending back over.

But Kitty jumps up and wraps her arms round the splendid monument. "No! Take it myself." Staggering with it, she bobs her head in to pluck a macaron with her chipped teeth.

"Can you manage?" asks Biermont.

Kitty flexes her wings and nods back, hovering off with the enormous sweet. She leads them through the open gates and zigzags into the Palace, humming down the corridor to the hatch of the chamber. "In there," she says, extracting another macaron as she sets down. Nudging the big megaphone with her elbow, she calls, "Hallo?"

"*Ça va*?" adds my boy. "Are you okay?"

"Moojag!" Charlie calls back up.

Kitty bends over to pull a wand with her teeth from her tutu's waist band. She waves it over a sensor pad, releasing the hatch. Moojag grins, clasping his hands. "Bravo, Kitty, I do believe the macarons have given you a super boost. Take another." She almost loses her grip on the tower, doing a twirl as Moojag kneels down with Biermont to peer into the dark chamber.

"Hurry," blurts Nema, "the marshmallow's expanding."

Moojag glances at Biermont. "I'll go down. You two watch-keep." Kitty nods to herself. Busily scoffing her seventh cookie, she barely notices him hover upside down and dive in.

Moojag lowers himself inside the chamber until his hat's letters almost touch the bubbling sticky surface. "Clutch to my hand!"

Izzy's twitching eyes struggle to roll up. "Take her first," calls Charlie. They all wade in toward Izzy, bucking her up high enough so that Moojag can grip her wrists.

Izzy spits out the marshmallow gunk as he pulls her up. "Grab my feet," she calls down. Nema reaches for the ankles dangling through the hatch and holds on tight as Moojag clamps himself to the door. He raises his legs, flipping up and over, super cicada muscles bulging under his clothes. He hauls out Izzy and Nema followed by Adam and Charlie, each having locked on to the other and landing with a thump in a big heap.

Charlie wheezes, rolling over, and wipes the marshmallow from her silky sleeves. "Time to get you all back to RW."

"Me too," mumbles a floating frustum of macarons.

"Kitty, is that you?" asks Charlie.

"Mm-hmm," answers the Pof, tottering behind the remaining two-thirds of the showstopper. "And my two prizes."

"All the power you need to get to the Real World, huh?"

"*Lots* more."

"And Poof Poof?"

Kitty gobbles down another cookie. "Okay, I be back soon to visit mummy."

Moojag lowers the coat to reveal his sunken wings. "Aldon expelled me from the lab."

Charlie reaches out, but he flinches and quickly hikes the coat back up over his shoulders. "You are *perfect* just as you are."

Yes, my love, you really are.

Moojag lets the jacket drop a little and flits to Charlie's side, locking his arms around her.

"You don't have to hide your wings anymore," says Nema. "In RW, you can be yourself."

"We have to get the Auts out quick," says Izzy, fidgeting, "before those meanies get back."

"She's right," says Biermont, "we need to move. I'll rush back to get them ready. Moojag, will you come?"

Silence...

Charlie turns to Kitty. "I should really regret if all the Pofs were left behind." Kitty frowns at Moojag, shrugging her wings. He rocks his head and glances round at Biermont.

Nema nods. "It's okay, we'll tell them all about our 'sweet fruits'."

"We can try," says Adam. "We've nothing to lose."

"Only our lives," hisses Izzy.

"Would you like to stay here, while we go to the Pofs?" Izzy peers down the dark corridor and shakes her head.

Moojag inspects his pocket-watch, swerving round after Biermont. "Dare not be late, Charlie," he calls back, rolling his eyes and waving the watch from its gold chain as he hovers away. "The Auts expect you at 15:26 and 14 seconds. Not a second later; not a second sooner..."

32

COSTUME CAROUSEL

Kitty zips from the chamber down the dim corridor with the others chasing after. "Costumes, this way."

"Is that where you keep your clothes?" asks Izzy.

Kitty halts as they enter the bright hall and looks back, eyes sparkling. "Be anyone you like!"

Nema looks at Adam. "Masking?"

"Probably."

"Sounds like more waste to me," says Izzy.

Kitty looks down and crosses her arms over her belly. "Resources," explains Adam.

Kitty's eyes widen. "*Cheese* sauce?"

"Re-sources—"

"Oh, sugar!"

Adam frowns. "No, not in RW, anyway."

"Natural sugars are really good for you," says Nema, "in

small doses, but too much is harmful."

Izzy pouts, patting her deflated pouch as Kitty props open the thick red curtains dividing the room. "Ah, sweet fruit."

Nema nods, passing through to a large space filled with dozens of little winged people darting about. The Pofs are changing out of their show costumes and filing them away on velvet hangers in a giant revolving carousel. Rainbow rows of colour-coordinated garments shift round with children dipping in and out as it turns.

Charlie approaches a lone Pof with fiery-red hair and upward-pointing eyes. The poised girl stands proudly in her orange bikini beside the carousel's controls.

"Stop the machine please, dear Rania! We must talk to you all urgently."

The girl glances at Kitty before depressing a push button switch and waving down the Pofs. Nema and Izzy shield their ears from the screeching motor, as it comes to a halt, and gaze at the humongous swaying wardrobe that stretches right up to the ceiling.

"Gather round, my dears," Charlie calls. "You see these lovelies? They have come from the world overground." The Pofs look the RWs up and down, and gasp. "They've come to tell you how wonderful it is. And if you like how it sounds, we'll go and live up there together!"

Kitty hops forward and tells them all about real fruits and ve-ge-ta-bles.

"What about our candy?" asks Rania. She pinches Izzy's skin and cackles as it vibrates. "How will we eat? Who will give us these fruits?"

"In RW, we have all we need," says Adam. "There's plenty for everyone. You just take whatever you want."

"We swap, too," says Nema.

"Swap?"

"Yes. I give you an avocado, and you, say…give me a banana."

Rania cocks her head. "Give me a banana."

"*Or*," adds Izzy, "you give a small bag of zapped mushrooms, and I give…a whole pineapple."

Deja, the barrier Pof, leaps out smirking from the huddled group. Charlie smiles at the girl. "Ah yes, your favourite."

"It's sweet," adds Nema, "but it's also *real* and real juicy."

Adam nods. "And it has your vital vitamin C, manganese, and thiamin," he says, "keeping you strong and full of energy."

"Helps you digest too," says Izzy, patting her achy, candy-filled stomach. "So you won't get a sore tum."

"Sweets that'll never drain your energy," adds Nema, "or make you blue."

"That's good," whispers a little Pof, nuzzling into the nook of Charlie's arm. "I only really like orange."

"Of course you do," says Charlie, caressing the girl's fine amber ringlets.

The Pofs nod, high-fiving each other excitedly. "But," mutters a small one lurking by the carousel, wings hidden between the folds of a costume, "we're different." Kitty hovers over to stroke the boy's wing and gazes back at Charlie.

"Your wings are beautiful," says Nema.

"We *know* that, but they won't work up there." Rania shudders. "They'll shrivel up…go soft in the wind and rain."

"We could get EATEN," squeals Deja.

"They *know* they're human, right?" whispers Izzy.

"I don't think they're sure *what* they are," says Nema.

Adam nudges his friends and steps forward. "You won't come to any harm, because you *are* human. And anyway, if you came to live with us, your wings would be healthier than ever. Maybe you could even learn to fly."

The Pofs hover closer and check their wings, muttering to themselves. "We're not like you," sighs Deja, pretending to pick floss off her tutu.

Adam explains how everyone in RW is free and treated equally.

"You could hover wherever you like," says Nema. "The sun always shines, and the air is cleaner and fresher than it's ever been." She checks herself for fibbing. *It IS very clean, though, cleaner than pre-Surge air.* "There are lush, green forests; pretty butterflies and birds; and flowers—all colours of the rainbow. And lots of magical forest to explore…"

33

15:26:14

Poof Poof zooms into the lab to warn Aldon about the Real Worlders. "The traitors have escaped," she calls, panting.

"What do you mean, 'they ESCAPED'?"

Brix and Travis tut at her, shaking their heads, while Sparkles takes Sparky's hand and squeezes it tight.

Poof Poof peers round at the lifeless Auts. "Someone or some*thing* got them out."

Aldon turns to scan them and fixes his unblinking eyes on Sparkles. "Where is MOOJAG?"

Sparkles rocks her head as Brix turns to Aldon and whispers in his ear, "You ousted him from the lab, remember?"

"I *know*, you twit," Aldon snaps. "Just testing the scrawny rat."

"Of course."

Aldon thwacks his cane on the ground, making Poof Poof

trip over herself as she scuttles backwards.

"Well, what are you waiting for, you *annoying* little woman? Go find the aliens before they do any *more* damage." Poof stumbles and hovers out through the Switching Room for Pof Palace.

***

Charlie checks her watch while the Pofs gawk at the strangers' brilliant skins. "It's decision time. Will you join us, or will you stay down here with the conniving Conqip?"

"What was *that*?" whispers Izzy. She sticks her nose in the air and sniffs the tail of a fading scent: sweet like berries, yet musty like sweaty arm pits. "Can you smell *off*-blueberries?"

Kitty darts to the curtains and pokes her head through as a door slams shut. She glares back at Charlie. "Mummy!"

"If Poof Poof heard us," says Charlie, "she'll be headed straight for Aldon."

"It's 15:21!" warns Adam.

"Right. Come on everyone." Charlie lifts back the heavy curtain and charges out. "It's now or never." Nema and her friends chase her across the hall, wondering what it actually means to be late. Of course, there's no such thing in the Real World.

"What if we don't make it by 15:*26*?" asks Adam.

"Hate to think." Charlie flings open the front door. "Any kind of change completely messes up an Aut's flow. They live for routine. Once, they refused to work for a whole month, even with Aldon confiscating their music."

Kitty buzzes through the iron gates with her friend Rania.

"Only two Pofs coming," Nema calls ahead.

"We tried," says Charlie, waving everyone toward the Switching Room door. It releases to reveal Moojag hanging there upside down like a bat, his arms locked around him.

"15:26," he says, with a huff.

"And *14* seconds," retorts Charlie, pulling him in with her and marching over to URAQT. "Kitty, Rania—wait here. RWs—come with us. Moojag—where's Biermont?"

My rattled boy pats down his jacket sleeves as she releases him. "Monty left when the meanies returned."

34

EXAUTUS

Charlie and the friends enter the lab to find all the Auts seated back at their stations. No sound but the dizzying drone of computers choking the stuffy room.

Izzy gasps at the indifferent teens. "How come they aren't ready?"

Moojag traipses in, tapping his watch, "15:28, Charlie." He shakes his head, burying it in his hands. Nema reaches out, but he flinches.

"You're too late," says Sparkles, flopping down from her station. She hobbles over and points up to the discoloured patch on the wall.

"The Conqip took down your banner?" asks Izzy.

Sparkles shrugs. "They know your plan. They said we'd never survive up *there*."

"You know they're lying again, right?" asks Adam.

The muddled Aut shakes her head and glances away, flicking her fingers.

Charlie smiles reassuringly at Moojag and turns to the workers. "Dear SuperAuts, what I shall say is very important. The Conqip ARE right." All heads jolt up. "You ARE different." They turn to each other and gasp. "We ALL are different." They tut, gazing back at their screens.

"I think what Charlie is saying," says Nema, "is that we're all unique in our own way."

The Auts frown as Sparky wanders stiffly over to join his sister and the strangers. "They said they'd take away our music *forever*," Sparkles explains.

Nema shakes her head. "You need to be with people who understand, who care how you feel." Sparkles and Sparky nod, gaping back at their dazed friends. "People who let you eat when you want, let you create when you feel inspired. A place you can listen to music whenever you like."

A tall Aut lurking in the corner springs up punching his bony fist in the air. "That's right," says Adam. "Don't let those bullies control you." The Auts glare back at him and his daring words. "They only treat you like this because *they* are weak."

"And that's not power," adds Nema, wrestling with all the thoughts in her head. "It's control. Real power is knowing yourself and what you need."

"The Conqip don't even care about themselves," says Adam. Sparky peers up at him and shrugs his shoulders. "They drink all day and stuff their gobs with candy, *and* real food - I bet they never shared any of that with you."

Nema sticks her hands on her hips. "They don't have anything better to do than insult the rest of us. When was the last time they showed any interest in *you*?"

Moojag gazes up at his sister and wonders about her life up there in the perfect Real World. *Would they really accept me? They're all different, sûr, but none of them have wings like me. What AM I? Not like them OR the Pofs, and certainly nothing like a Conqip. Will Dad really still want me when he finds I have wings? Maybe I'm only good for this place after all.*

"But could we be happier in RW?" asks Sparkles.

"We can't promise it," says Charlie. "But I do know that, as long as you are true to yourself, no one can stop you trying."

"We could stay *here* and try," suggests Sparkles.

"You could. But would it be worth always having to stand up to those dragons? Skip all the nastiness and go somewhere full of love that's already home."

"Not a Conqip in sight," says Nema, looking at Moojag.

"Sunlight, fresh oxygen, and real food. *Real* life."

"You can trust us," says Charlie. "Can you trust the Conqip?"

Sparky leaps forward and draws the letter S down his chest with his fist.

"You *are* SUPER. You're not called the SuperAuts for nothing." Charlie turns pointing to the Switching Room door. "I'm sorry. I know we were late this time, but your lives will be easier from now on, I promise. And I do believe you are ready to be mighty. Come with us now, before Aldon returns, and we'll get you out safely."

Sparkles turns to lightly hug her brother. "Can we have lizard skins, too?"

"Of course," answers Charlie, "and you know what? They were actually designed to help people manage their feelings."

Sparky strokes Adam's leg and gives him a thumbs up. "They've stopped working down here," says Nema, "but when we get back out, they'll light up and Hola; even change temperature if it's too hot or too cold. You'll never want to take yours off."

"You don't *need* to," exclaims Izzy.

Sparkles frowns and pokes Izzy's middle. "What if you want to urinate?"

"You just pee, then you can drink it too."

Sparky pouts, shaking his head.

"PIE purifies," Adam explains. "Turns your pee straight back into clean water. *All* your bodily fluids get recycled."

Sparky and Sparkles giggle. "PIE purifies, PIE purifies… You RWs might actually be weirder than us," says Sparkles. Izzy bows. The Auts cheer and gather round the RWs to inspect their colourful skins.

"Okay," says Charlie, "this is what we're going to do. As you pass through the Switching Room, you will receive a pair of goggles, which you must wear to protect your eyes from the sun—"

"Will we go *blind* if we don't?" asks Sparkles.

"No, but better to be safe, since your eyes will be sensitive to the light for the first few days. In twos, you will pass into the Switching Room and go directly to door PG. I know you're not allowed in there, but today you have my special permission. It may feel strange at first, but it's super soft."

The Auts gawk at each other and back at her. "No—it's not like the marshmallow chamber. You don't sink; you just pass straight through to Porto Gajoom. A chute will drop down from the oculus in the ceiling, just like the tunnel into the factory. This will scoot you up to level zero; then you'll take another into the lighthouse. We will meet there and leave Gajoomdom together, forever."

Moojag circles the room, coaxing out the last dithering Auts as Charlie directs the first lot into the Switching Room. Sparkles tuts at one boy lingering behind another tall one. She points to a peculiar bulge projecting from the Aut's middle. He sighs, pulling a computer from his tracksuit bottoms. Sparky catches another Aut sneaking two pairs of headphones under her sweater.

"Will we need *these* up there?" asks Sparkles, grabbing a pair and stringing it up.

"I'm not sure they'd work," says Nema. "But it's quiet in RW, and you can play music through your PIE hood, so—"

"You can wear them for the journey," says Charlie. "I will sign if anything important needs communicating. We won't need computers, anyway, when we have PIE."

The Aut smiles, popping the defenders back over her ears and placing her friend's over his. The remaining Auts shuffle into the Switching Room, grabbing a pair of goggles from Charlie and trailing over to the marshmallow wall.

"You're not *actually* Aut, are you?" says Sparkles, eyeing Moojag with a set smile. "'Cause I've seen you, you know, using your wings."

"It is true; I can hover. But I do Aut things too."

Sparky, last in from the lab, shuts the door looking at

Moojag and circles a fist around his chest.

"We're sorry, Moojag," adds Sparkles. "It's just, we've *always* been Auts, you know?"

"I have *always* been Aut, too—just with wings."

Sparkles steps into the marshmallow with her brother. "Good luck, Aut-Pof," she calls as they're sucked from the room.

Maybe they're right. I'm just an erratic Pof, not even a real Aut. No one will get me in RW. Anyway, I'd be like prey up there in the wild.

My girl steps over to Moojag. He opens his mouth to speak, but no word makes it out alive. "It's a big change," she says nodding, "but we'll help you. And Dad, well, he won't believe it at first, but—" Moojag frowns, peering at Charlie waving them on.

"Nem," calls Adam, "let's go!"

"Hang on," says Nema. She's not sure what to say to her brother. They've been apart for so long. If only they had more time.

Charlie nudges Kitty and Rania over to the wall. "Sweet Pofs, you'd better go next, then."

"KITTY POOF!!!" calls a shrill voice. *"CHARLIE! WHAT HAVE YOU DONE WITH MY KITTY!?"*

Kitty darts behind Rania and tries latching onto her tutu, but her nervy friend shimmies away. Poof Poof charges into the Switching Room and whizzes past Charlie to her skulking girl, now partially hidden behind the RWs.

"You can't go with *them*," Poof Poof cries, darting left and right.

"I *can*."

"You're a POF," she squeals, snatching for Kitty. "You belong to ME."

"She's decided to return to RW," says Charlie.

Poof Poof barges past her, nostrils flaring. "Out of my way!" she cries, dropping beside her daughter. "Candy, darling?" she whispers. Kitty steps out, lured by the bucket full of treats hanging off Poof Poof's arm. She glances at her mother's beady bloodshot eyes, glaring at her through the skewed spectacles. She drops her head and peers round at Charlie.

"You confused my poor baby," snarls Poof, pumping her fists. "We *cannot* survive up there!"

"We *can*," gulps Kitty. She squints to trap her welling tears and points to Nema. "*She's* right."

Poof Poof turns to my girl and jabs her shoulder with a sticky wand. "Do *you* have wings, girl?" Nema shakes her head. "Then what would *you* know about our survival?"

Nema shakes her head again, turning to Adam.

"RW is really very safe," he says. "Safer than down here, and Kitty will have the best carers, and PIE too."

Poof Poof jabs Adam hard in the kneecaps and grabs her daughter by the wrist. "Kitty will STARVE!" She drags her wriggling and kicking across the floor towards door T42. "You too, Rania."

"Mummy *is* right…" resigns Kitty. She squeezes the tears out of her eyes and shakes them off.

"ALL THOSE DELICIOUS SWEET FRUITS," calls Izzy after them, "HONEY AND CAROBS, TOO!"

Kitty yanks her arm from her mother's grip. "NO. *They* are right!"

Poof Poof stamps her foot, sending Kitty scrambling back over to Charlie. The corners of her mouth sink as she drops to her knees and clasps her hands. "Don't *leave* me, Kitty."

"Come with us, Poof Poof," insists Charlie. "It's not safe for you here now."

Poof Poof jerks a hand in the air, as though back-swatting a fly. "Do as you WANT," she says, turning away. "I don't care."

Kitty wavers. "I miss you…with all my heart."

"Hmmm."

"I *do*," cries Kitty, peering out the corner of her eye.

Izzy tugs my girl's arm, pointing to the flickering Spondylux. Nema mutters "RW" into her shell and steps softly over to the irritable little woman. Poof Poof squints over her specs as pictures of the Real World and real food beam out in front of her.

Charlie steps to Poof Poof's side as she turns away. "You realise they won't supply you anymore when they find out you let the Auts go."

Poof Poof scowls as her stomach rumbles. "They would *never*." Charlie turns back to the RWs, directing them to the marshmallow wall as Poof Poof turns for door T42.

"*POOF POOF!*" Aldon's roaring voice echoes from Pof Palace.

Charlie grabs the dithering RWs. "Go. NOW."

"See you up there, Moojag," calls Izzy. Moojag holds a hand to his chest and bows.

"Come on, Nem," calls Adam, plunging into the pink mass with Izzy.

Nema pokes her foot in, then pulls it back out and turns to Moojag. "You *are* coming, aren't you?"

Moojag looks up at her. "Goodbye."

"You're staying, for the Pofs?" Moojag nods. "Gran

designed the Gajoom skin, didn't she?" He nods again with a wink. "And *you* invented the Gajoom? That's how you got your new name. MOOJAG is GAJOOM spelled backwards, isn't it?"

He smiles nodding, before losing himself in more goodbyes she doesn't recognise, *"Totsiens, kwaheri, wadaeaan, vaarwel, alavida, hüvastu…"*

"Don't say goodbye, say Gajoom," she says, turning to step inside the wall.

Charlie throws an arm out to Poof Poof. "Come, let us leave now—together." Kitty takes her mum's quivering hand and places it over Charlie's. Poof Poof clasps it tight and swings an arm around her Kitty as Charlie grabs hold of Rania, and they make for the wall.

Moojag watches them all leap through the marshmallow, leaving him alone with only the barking voices of Aldon and his squad bounding into the deserted lab. *"POOF POOF! WHERE ARE MY AUTS?!"*

AUT TO STAY, OR AUT TO GO

"Hello or *no*?"

Moojag spins back round to find the man jumping out of the marshmallow wall. "What are *you* doing down here?"

Wats wipes the pink gunk from his sleeves. "You've got a ticket to ride, sir!" Moojag rolls his eyes. "Nema is your sister!"

"*Je sais*."

"Well, if you *know*, what you still doin' here, friend?"

Moojag throws down his jacket and rocks his head, flapping his dishevelled wings. "I'm not an Aut, Wats. I thought I was. Now I'm not sure *what* I am. Or who I must *be*."

"It's okay, we can work it out…Indeed you *are* an Aut. *And* a Pof. A Neurodivergent, too! But you're also Moojag, and a Moojag's got to do what a Moojag's got to do."

My boy glares at the man and sighs. "You're here, there, and everywhere," chants Wats. "You gotta follow your lonely heart, goo goo Gajoom—"

"*WHERE ARE MY AUTS!? YOU STUPID...*"

Wats grabs Moojag's hands and glances up at the ceiling. "When you're done down here, kid, just get back up there. And don't ever change, okay?" He releases Moojag and skips in reverse, sinking bum-first back into the marshmallow. "I say goodbye, *you* say?"

"Gajoom," sighs my sweet Aut-Pof.

Wats mouths 'hello', waving goodbye as his body dissolves into the wall, and the door of the lab finally releases. Moojag darts into WC and hauls himself over the toilet rim, just as a fuming Aldon marches into the Switching Room.

"YOU will pay for this!" Aldon yells at Brix, slamming the door closed behind them.

"But I didn't—"

"SHUT IT."

***

Finally tumbling out of a porthole from the lighthouse, Charlie and the three Pofs are greeted by the RWs. Phil is there, too, on Myrta with all the dizzy Auts gazing out to sea and up at the real blue sky.

"Hello or *no*?" Nema shakes her head at Izzy and turns to Wats peering in her face. "Your Moojag isn't coming," he declares with a flick of the wrist. "He's torn."

"What do you mean?" asks Izzy.

Wats spins round, "Well, my dear Wizard of Iz, I believe he feels the need to rescue his Pof cousins. You get my gist?"

"But he can't do it on his own?" says Adam.

"Well, we all need a little help from our friends. He's a real nowhere man. If only he had something to protect him from the meanies, a some*one* too."

Nema's afraid she *does* get his meaning. *I wish people would stop talking in riddles*, she thinks. *He means ME, doesn't he? But what can I do? The Pofs wouldn't come. Biermont's still down there, though, so my brother will be fine. Won't he?*

"Deja," Poof Poof croaks, sneaking up behind her.

"Deja?" asks Nema.

"She will come if you take her a *real* pineapple. And where Deja goes, the others follow."

"Does Moojag know?" asks Adam.

Poof Poof scrunches up her nose. "Of course not, boy. He's an *Aut*."

"*Actually*—" says Izzy.

"PHIL!" Nema calls up to the floater.

"Yes, lovely?"

"Any spare PIEs?"

"No, girl," he answers grinning as Sparkles and Sparky stroke his twinkling chin. "These fine teens nabbed the lot." The giggling siblings, in their new multi-coloured skins, dart over to the other Auts surrounded by a bunch of holograms.

"Take *this*, though!" Phil hollers, lobbing Nema a small pineapple.

"Thanks!" She winces catching the spiky fruit and looks her friends up and down. Adam nods.

"What?" Izzy sighs, checking her freshly charged, glowing turquoise skin.

"PIEs." Nema holds out her hand. "'Designed to free the people; tougher than any armour ever invented'."

Izzy gawks at Adam whipping off his PIE skin. "All right," she says pouting and reluctantly peeling back her hood, "but don't lose it!" Sparky and Sparkles chuck their track suits overboard for Adam and Izzy.

"Bring back Nem too, please—" Adam pulls on the bottoms as my girl dashes back to the lighthouse with the pineapple and their PIEs.

***

Moojag dives into the swirling water and down the giant drain, rolling out into a puddle at the foot of a Gajoom. "It's *me*," says the ex-Conqip wriggling his feet out of the disguise.

My boy scrambles to pick himself up and flicks the water off his hat. "They've gone, Monty."

"*Takiwātanga*, my friend. When the time is right."

Moojag nods, shuddering his damp wings and donning his hat as they veer onto the candy path. Hopping over the crisscross pave stones, he wonders whether the other Pofs feel anything like he does. *At least, we LOOK the same.* He stops for a moment with Biermont to watch something loom in the distance. It's a little Gajoom bounding toward them at super speed.

Moojag hovers up, throwing his arms about in the air, "Where are you going, *petit* stick?" The Gajoom stalls in its tracks before them and stomps on the spot. Moojag covers his delicate ears from its incessant thudding and stumbles back as it leaps forward. It hurdles over them and bolts off, but now there's another great big throbbing one also heading their way.

Ga-joooom…STIK!

Biermont glares at the taller, bulgier Gajoom drawing near. UNWRAPPED and SPROUTING.

Ga-joooom...STIK! Ga-joooom...STIK! Ga-joooom... STIK!

They leap out of the irate Gajoom's way and wait for it to bolt past with its three agitated little clones. "Worry not," says Biermont. "The Auts are freed, and we'll sort these missed Gajooms in a flash."

Moojag stands tall, gazing up at the patchy scarlet sky. Somehow he's not afraid. He no longer feels alone. He's safe now, because he knows he has the neurodivergents waiting for him up there, and he's officially a Pof now too.

My boy senses my presence. I want to pull him in close. I reach out...

Mum?

Yes, my love...

If that's really you, you should know—your boy isn't lost. I've been down here all along. And I forgive you; I know you tried your best. Did you know I'm a Pof? Send me a sign, anything, so I know everything will be all right.

Yes, my darling. I've been here all along, too, watching

over you. I'm so proud of my sweet, clever boy. Trust your intuition, my love; the rest will follow. Just keep being *you*.

Biermont cocks his head. "Did you hear that? Someone calling your real—"

"Mum?"

Goodbye, my love. Your sister is here now.

"MONZI!" Moojag swings round and grins at my glistening, silver body sprinting toward him with a pineapple clamped under my left arm and two gleaming PIEs draped over my right. "Happy unbirthday, dear brother, Monzi!" I present him with a Victoria sponge cake and nod to Biermont. "Let's go rescue those Pofs!"

Hello or *no?*...

If you enjoyed
MOOJAG,
get the full cast
audiobook
and **ebook**
too!

Review Moojag

Why not share what you thought of this book with
other readers. Leave a review on the website of the store
where you bought it, at www.goodreads.com, and all over
whatsnapchatvibeinstatwitface...
@moojagbook @spondyluxpress
#moojag #gajoom

Subscribe to:
WWW.MOOJAG.COM
for news, fun stuff and the chance to
WIN a Gajoomdom TREAT! *(Chip chop, though - before the
greedy Conqip munch the lot!)*